WINED AND DIED

A HOME CRAFTING MYSTERY

WINED AND DIED

CRICKET MCRAE

**WHEELER
CHIVERS**

This Large Print edition is published by Wheeler Publishing, Waterville, Maine, USA and by AudioGO Ltd, Bath, England.
Wheeler Publishing, a part of Gale, Cengage Learning.

The text of this Large Print edition is unabridged.
Other aspects of the book may vary from the original edition.
Set in 16 pt. Plantin.

LIBRARY OF CONGRESS CATALOGING-IN-PUBLICATION DATA

McRae, Cricket.
  Wined and died : a home crafting mystery / by Cricket McRae.
    p. cm. — (Wheeler Publishing large print cozy mystery)
  ISBN-13: 978-1-4104-4075-4 (softcover)
  ISBN-10: 1-4104-4075-3 (softcover)
    1. Women artisans—Fiction. 2. Murder—Investigation—Fiction.
  3. Large type books. I. Title.
PS3613.C58755W56 2011b
813'.6—dc22   2011024200

BRITISH LIBRARY CATALOGUING-IN-PUBLICATION DATA AVAILABLE

Published in 2011 in the U.S. by arrangement with Midnight Ink, an imprint of Llewellyn Publication, Woodbury, MN 55125-2989 USA.
Published in 2012 in the U.K. by arrangement with Llewellyn Worldwide Limited.

U.K. Hardcover: 978 1 445 86548 5 (Chivers Large Print)
U.K. Softcover: 978 1 445 86549 2 (Camden Large Print)

Printed in the United States of America
1 2 3 4 5 6 7 15 14 13 12 11

ACKNOWLEDGMENTS

Thanks once more to family and friends who encourage me at every stage of creating a novel. Special thanks to Kevin for putting up with me as deadlines approach and for setting up a cozy place in his recording studio where I can escape. My writing buddies Mark and Bob are consistently on my side while at the same time keeping me in line. The folks in various writing organizations — Sisters in Crime, Mystery Writers of America, and Northern Colorado Writers — provide more inspiration than they know. And I'm so grateful for the skilled support of the team at Midnight Ink: Terri Bischoff, Connie Hill, Lisa Novak, Courtney Colton, and Donna Burch.

Amy Lockwood and Bob Binckes introduced me to their homemade mead fermented with champagne yeast. If it weren't for them I'd never have known honey wine could be so crisp and dry. Dr. Jane Bock, writer and forensic botanist extraordinaire, offered advice on herbs and wild and poisonous plants. Jenny Luper at the Redstone Meadery in Boulder, Colorado showed me how a meadery functions and answered myriad questions with patience and expertise. Paul Slaughter provided vital information regarding the ins and outs of a psychotherapy practice. As always, I take full blame for anything I got wrong.

In vino veritas
(in wine is truth)
— *Pliny, the Elder*

ONE

"Sophie Mae, what does it mean to know someone in the biblical sense?"

Erin's question caught me mid-swallow. I snorted and spluttered while waving back Barr's attempt to rescue me from death by vanilla latte. Finally I managed to stop coughing long enough to say, *"What?"*

My housemate's eleven-year-old daughter sat back on the sofa and considered me with gray eyes that were far too wise in her elfin face. "Wow. It must be good."

I reached for a tissue and dabbed at my eyes. "Where did you hear that?" Somehow I doubted the outdated phrase had suddenly become part of the normal sixth-grade vernacular.

She opened her mouth. Hesitated. Closed it.

Alarm bells clanged in my head. "Erin, what have you been up to?"

"It's okay. You don't have to tell me. I'll

just look it up on the Internet." She stood.

"No!" Who knew what sites searching the phrase "to know in the biblical sense" would take her to, whatever parental control software was on her computer.

Erin stopped. Smiled. Waited.

I waffled, mentally scrambling for what to tell her.

Barr had moved over by the fireplace and watched our little exchange with an amused curve to his lips. Now he weighed in. "It means to have sex."

Her face fell. "Oh. Is that all? I thought it might be something interesting." She turned toward the hallway that led to her bedroom.

"Not so fast." I cleared my throat and sipped my latte, savoring the sweet, tepid liquid. Barr and Erin had stopped at Beans R Us on the way home from school and picked up my favorite. "I still want to know where you heard it."

Barr was right. I'd overreacted when she'd asked the question, but the little imp had so smoothly sidestepped my question that my curiosity now insisted on an answer. An answer that would no doubt be just as boring as the one she'd just heard from Barr. I hoped.

She sighed and flopped back down on the sofa. "It was on one of the tapes."

My face squinched in confusion. "Tapes?"

"The ones Barr got at Granny's Attic on Sunday. There's a lady talking about someone who knows a bunch of people in the biblical sense."

Ohmygod.

Two days earlier I'd agreed to take a break from filling orders for Winding Road Bath Products and get out of the house for the afternoon. It was a rare sunny spring Saturday in Cadyville. First a brisk bike ride along the path by the river, then lunch at the River Otter Diner, followed by a search for the perfect bargain at Granny's Attic Thrift.

My housemate, Meghan Bly, was spending the week in New Jersey with her long-distance beau, and my new husband and I had taken over responsibility for her daughter while she was on vacation.

At the thrift store Barr had discovered a cardboard box filled with a dozen or so mini-cassettes. I'd peered inside. "You're kidding, right?"

Barr glanced up at me. "Remember the Morton case the judge threw out because the department's digital recorder didn't catch the whole confession?"

"Yeah . . ."

"That won't happen again. Ever since then, I've used the department's recorder plus my personal cassette recorder. Getting harder to find this size of tape anymore, though. These look to be in good shape. I'll just record over them."

I left him to it. Barr was one of two detectives on the tiny Cadyville police force. That particular case had involved a drug dealer at the local high school. The guy had gotten off with a stern talking to instead of the deserved jail time. No wonder he wanted those tapes.

I hadn't thought about it again.

Until now.

"Where are they?" I asked Erin.

She looked out the window at the light mist smudging the afternoon air. Mumbled something.

"Excuse me?"

"In my room."

"Bug, those aren't yours. They're for Barr's work. You had no right to take them, forget actually listening to them." I stood.

Practically leaping to her feet, she said, "I'll get them."

Nuh-uh. Too cooperative. I followed her to her room.

Erin was a great kid, and honest, too. But

12

she was also smart as the dickens, and growing increasingly bored by school. Meghan had been considering the middle school counselor's suggestion that Erin skip a grade, but questioned whether it would be beneficial in the long run. In the meantime, we encouraged Erin to develop interests outside of her usual schoolwork. So far she'd tried playing the guitar, learning tennis, and studying for Junior Jeopardy. Nothing had stuck.

When Barr and I got married, we renovated the house I had shared with Meghan and Erin for several years. Now there was a tiny, top floor apartment for us newlyweds, and new bedrooms on the main floor for the Bly girls. I followed Erin down the short hallway to hers. Gone were the puffy purple comforter and pile of stuffed animals that had populated her childhood bed for years, replaced by the expanse of a log cabin quilt in shades of blue that her great-grandmother had given her. The walls and ceiling were the palest indigo. Built-in bookshelves and shadow boxes displaying her considerable collection of bookmarks had replaced pastel prints of kittens and puppies.

Her desk overlooked the backyard gardens and chicken pen. The cardboard box sat on the chair, Barr's mini-cassette recorder on top. She handed it to me without meeting my eyes.

I ejected the tape from the recorder and turned it over. *36B* was handwritten on the label in pencil. Not a bra size, I hoped. I counted eleven tapes in the box. The first one had no label at all. Neither did the next one. Then I found one marked *42R*. Huh. The others were blank, until I dug out the last tape: *228T.* What were these things?

"Did you listen to all of them?" I asked, arranging the cases so they all faced the same way.

"Most of them don't have anything on them. The one you took out of the player was the first one with someone talking. I didn't get to the other ones with the numbers and letters on them." She didn't sound happy to have missed out, either.

I looked up to see Erin eyeing the box. "What possessed you to listen to these in the first place?"

She shrugged. "I thought they might have ideas."

Oh, Lord. "Ideas for what?"

"For my book."

"Your book."

A nod. "I've decided to write a book." She pointed to a red spiral notebook on the desk. "I'm taking lots of notes."

14

"What kind of a book?"

"That's what I'm trying to figure out." The *duh* was implied.

"Well, if anyone can do it, you can. But those tapes are out. You'll just have to get ideas like everyone else."

"How's that?"

"Using your powers of observation," I said. Even I could detect the lofty note in my voice. Like I knew how to write a book.

"That's what I was doing." Sullen.

"Yes. Well." Not much more I could say to that. Thing was, I didn't want her "observing" anything inappropriate for a tween girl.

"But —"

"No buts. You should be doing your homework."

She glared at me.

"Don't give me a hard time just because your mom isn't here."

"Fine." She turned her back to me and started jerking books and papers out of her backpack.

As I passed by Barr in the living room on my way up to our digs, I hissed at him. "I thought you took these upstairs."

"I left them in the entryway so I'd be sure to take them to work with me." Utterly unapologetic.

I stopped at the foot of the stairs. "Then

why didn't you?"

"Didn't see them."

"Right."

"Probably because they'd already migrated to the Bug's room."

Oh. "Good point."

Upstairs in our tidy sitting room, I considered the small tape player. Why would anyone talk about their sex life on tape? And what else had Erin heard? The thought made me cringe.

Nothing to do but find out for myself. I grabbed the three marked cases and Barr's recorder and headed down to my basement workroom.

TWO

The fragrance of meat slowly braising in the oven tantalized my senses as I made my way through the kitchen and down the narrow wooden staircase. In my workroom, I placed the box of tapes on the main work island and went to take stock of my outstanding orders as well as my current inventory. It looked like bath melts would be the best bet for this work session. They were simple to make so I could multitask without fear of messing up some delicate process, and quick, so I wouldn't be too long.

After gathering the ingredients and equipment to make the melts, I popped cassette *36B* — the one Erin had been listening to — into the player. I pushed *play* and began to measure hazelnut expeller oil and mango butter into a stockpot.

Sure enough, a woman on the tape began speaking about recent acts of sexual congress. But I detected air quotes around the

17

phrase "known in the biblical sense," and paused in my work to listen more closely.

"I advised the client that Internet dating was probably a bad idea for someone who is a self-professed sex addict," the woman's voice continued in a wry tone.

Great. Meghan would love that her daughter had listened to this. Maybe I should forget to mention Erin's mild foray into smut — at least while Meghan was gone. If she found out later, I could deal with it then. Old news is weak news.

But "client"? These weren't true confessions. Sure enough, as I listened, it soon became clear these were a therapist's verbal notes. Notes about a very private client session. How on earth had they turned up at the thrift store? I should just stop, call the therapist, and arrange to get the tapes back to her.

Except I didn't know who she was. And my guilt over what Erin might have heard overrode my guilt about invading a therapy client's privacy. I had a vested interest in Erin's well being, and that trumped an unidentified voice talking about people I didn't even know.

With growing relief I listened to the remaining comments about the sex addict. The therapist was short on detail and long on possible treatment options. None of it was graphic enough for me to worry about Erin's tender sensibilities — or her mother's. As I mixed citric acid and baking soda together in a two-gallon tub, the voice stopped and the tape whirred on, silent. I removed it and replaced it in the tiny plastic case.

Eyed the second tape.

I shouldn't. I really shouldn't. But what if Erin had fudged the truth? What if she'd listened to more than one?

228T was a minefield of vicarious pain relayed in the dispassionate monotone of a woman trying to figure out how to help her clients. First there were the notes about the strained relationship between two jealous sisters.

"Despite weekly sessions, I have yet to convince these women that since their mother died last year, continued competition for her affection is pointless."

I set out row upon row of molds and filled them with the salt mixture while learning the doctor's thoughts on how to treat a depressed teenager.

"The parents are urging medication, but the depression stems from his weight issues. I dislike treating the symptoms with drugs when the root of the problem is so evident."

As I listened, a hollow feeling settled into the pit of my stomach. Any curiosity or titillation had vanished. I had to admit that I liked the therapist's practical approach. As I poured the scented oils over the salt mixture in the molds, she began talking about a recent widower's grief.

"Seeking out professional help to get through the admittedly horrific processing of such a loss is admirable. He seems to be willing to let time do its job."

As someone who had suffered a similar loss, I knew exactly what she meant. I continued to fill the molds to the top as the voice spoke of a woman's debilitating terror of dogs and a man who'd recently been diagnosed with terminal cancer.

Finally it was over. It didn't seem like Erin could have stumbled into anything but the sadness of other people. That was enough, but manageable.

One left. *42R.* In for a penny, in for a pound.

The woman's shaking voice blared from the tiny speaker. Fear had displaced her earlier dispassion. I slid onto a stool, chin on one hand, listening hard.

"Today the client informed me murder is the only viable solution."

My hand crept over my lips, and I felt my

eyes go wide.

"Murder made to look like an accident or natural causes, so no suspicion will arise and no investigation will ensue. I cannot tell whether client is serious or pulling my chain like before. It doesn't matter. I can't take the chance. I explained that I'd have to adhere to the Statement of Understanding we agreed upon at the beginning of our sessions. That I'll be contacting the police. I think I'd better call the members of the Swenson family and warn them against one of their own, as well." A pause. The next words were lower but oozed stress. "The client didn't like it when I stated my intention to contact the authorities. Laughed at me for taking it seriously, and then slammed out the door, saying I'd regret it if I told anyone about our session. I need to talk to one of my colleagues about this."

Then, silence.

I waited.

Nothing. I sped through the tape, checking, straining to hear something that wasn't there.

I rewound it. Listened again. Confirmed that I'd heard right.

Murder.

Okay, wait a minute, Sophie Mae. The therapist said she'd contact the authorities and warn the victim. There was no reason to get all het up about it.

It had nothing to do with me.

Glancing at the clock, I was shocked to find how much time had gone by. Quickly, I finished pouring the last dozen bath melts and cleaned up. As I began to stack the cassettes back in their cardboard box, I spied something white against the brown cardboard. A thin strip of paper.

A debit card receipt, it turned out, printed in faded blue ink. And at the bottom: *Thank you for shopping with us, Elizabeth Moser.*

Up in the kitchen I put potatoes on to boil and dug the phone book out of its drawer. Elizabeth Moser was listed. She lived on Avenue A, not too far away. Was she the therapist on the tape? It didn't say in the phone book, just gave her name. I flipped to the yellow pages. No Elizabeth Moser under either Physicians or Psychotherapists.

If she wasn't the therapist, she might know who the person on the tape was. On the other hand, the receipt could have come from anywhere. Maybe it had nothing to do with the case.

Case? Now why did I have to go and think that?

No, Sophie Mae. No case.

■ ■ ■ ■

Barr leaned back in his chair and patted his stomach. "That dinner was delicious."

"Yeah," Erin said, and reached for another helping of mashed potatoes. At almost twelve years old, her ire was blessedly short lived.

I smiled. "There's carrot cake for dessert."

She returned the spoonful of potatoes to the serving bowl before it reached her plate. "With cream cheese frosting?"

I nodded.

"Yum!"

We were sitting around the butcher-block table in the kitchen amidst the ruins of a beef roast, mashed potatoes, and green beans. Pedestrian comfort food but good stuff. Brodie, Erin's old Pembroke Welsh corgi, lay with his head on her foot, angling for a tidbit.

"Can I eat my cake in my bedroom?" Erin asked.

"May I eat my cake in my bedroom," I corrected.

"Fine by me." She grinned.

"Smart aleck. Why?"

"History project's due at the end of the week."

"Well, don't make a habit of it."

"Okay." She took her plate to the sink while I cut a piece of cake. She left, and I slid back into my seat.

As soon as I heard music coming from her room, I leaned over the table toward Barr and whispered, "I need to talk to you."

"Can it wait? I need to go back to the office for a while."

I sat back. "You got a call?"

"No, nothing like that. Just have to catch up on a few things. I assumed you'd be working tonight anyway."

My lip quirked in regret. "Well, for a little while at least. I'm sorry I've been so busy lately. My new employee starts tomorrow. In just a few days we'll have more time together in the evenings, I promise."

In the beginning, Barr's work schedule had strained our relationship. Then the department had hired another detective, dramatically decreasing his overtime hours. Seven months into our marriage, a prime business opportunity had been dumped in my lap: a regional chain of natural food stores had decided to carry my entire line of Winding Road Bath Products. So just when the slow season should have been on the horizon, I was working like crazy to fill all their new orders in addition to those of

24

my regular wholesale clients and Internet retail customers.

I smiled at my husband. "Hard to complain about business being good."

Barr blinked. "What? Oh. Of course. I don't mind." Not exactly what a new bride wants to hear, but I didn't think it was personal.

"You seem distracted lately."

He pushed his chair back and stood. "Work stuff."

"That's vague." I reached for the carrot cake and a plate. "How much do you want?" At least I could find out if any therapists had contacted the department about violent clients while Barr had his dessert.

But he shook his head. "None for me. I'm full." And he turned and walked out of the kitchen.

Oh, dear. Barr Ambrose had just turned down my carrot cake. Not good.

Not good at all.

THREE

With Barr gone and Erin working away on her history project, I tried to put the tapes out of my mind and busy myself with processing Winding Road Internet orders from the last few days. But it was slow going since I kept staring at the computer screen and running the therapist's words over and over in my mind.

She'd mentioned warning the Swenson family. I didn't know any of them that well, but they owned the Grendel Meadery located northeast of Cadyville. I'd tasted their honey wine a few times in local restaurants but had never purchased a bottle. Quentin Swenson was the pharmacist at Kringle's Drugs. I knew him from the few prescriptions he'd filled for us over the years: bald, pasty, with an endless supply of cheerful yet meaningless chatter to ease the minds of the potentially ill folks he served on a daily basis. I knew his wife, Iris, better. She was a quilter and a new member of the recently reformed Cadyville Regional Artists Co-operative, or CRAC.

And another Swenson managed A Fine Body, the local wine shop. He'd helped me select wine for Meghan's birthday party a couple years before. I couldn't remember his name, but I certainly remembered the effect of his intense good looks on my solar plexus.

Ahem. That was before I'd met Barr, of course.

I thought there were a couple sisters, too, probably with different last names now. And there had been an article in the *Cadyville Eye* a while back about them. I ran an online search of the newspaper archives and found it. Nothing scandalous: over three years ago Grendel Meadery had successfully expanded into the international market. Which turned out to be Canada, specifically British Columbia, only a hundred miles or so north. The rest of the article went on to talk about how popular their mead was with the Canucks.

Booorring.

The Grendel website played hard on the Beowulf theme, gave a bit of information about mead, and served as a sales portal for shipping retail all over the United States and into Canada. It mentioned that it was a family-run business, but offered no details about the Swensons themselves.

I took a break and went up to check on Erin. She'd finished her homework for the night and was in bed reading. I gave her a goodnight hug and went in the kitchen. Forking carrot cake into my mouth with one hand, I looked up *Swenson* in the phone book. Dorothy, Glenwood, Quentin, and Willa were listed.

Back downstairs I drank tea and processed orders for another half an hour, until the front door opened and closed above. After a few moments, it became obvious Barr wasn't coming downstairs. He used to always announce his arrival home, but lately he'd been distant, standoffish. I tried to quash the icky feeling that thought gave me and quickly turned off my computer. The orders could darn well wait.

The bedside lamp in Erin's room was still on, but she'd fallen asleep. Brodie lay sprawled on his back on the quilt. His eyes opened to glittering slits when I walked in, then squeezed closed. I scratched his belly, turned off the light, checked the door locks, and headed up to our apartment.

"Do you know what this is?" I stood in our

bedroom doorway and held up the cassette marked *42R.*

From the bed, Barr glanced up at me over the top of his laptop screen. "None of your business?"

I entered the room and tossed the tape on the bed, along with the player. "Absolutely. But you know what else?"

He tapped a couple of keys and flipped the computer closed. The light from the bedside lamp accented a streak of gray at his temple and threw his curly chest hair into stark relief. Sexy, despite his obvious exhaustion.

"Do tell." He patted the mattress beside him.

I moved to perch on the side of the bed. "It's a psychotherapist's notes about her client sessions."

His lips twitched. "So they're *really* not any of your business."

I wiggled across him to my side of the bed and propped myself against the headboard. He reached for the recorder.

"Wait."

His hand froze.

"You've got to hear this."

"Nuh-uh." His chin swung back and forth. "No." But he withdrew his hand.

"Oh, hush. I tried to tell you about this

before you left for the station. Just listen." I pushed *play.*

Barr sighed. Gave me a look. But his eyes narrowed in concentration as he listened to the short recording. When it was over, he asked, "Is that it?"

"That's it."

"And . . ."

"And someone said they were going to kill someone and make it look like an accident. This therapist must have reported it. Do you remember anything like that?"

His head tipped to one side. "No one contacted us about this."

"Are you sure? Maybe a cadet or patrolman took the report."

"Possible murder? Robin and I would both have heard immediately." Robin being Detective Robin Lane.

"Uh-oh," I said.

"Any idea who this therapist is? The one talking on the tape?"

"I found a receipt with the name Elizabeth Moser at the bottom of the box, but she's not listed in the yellow pages. The only listing is residential."

The laptop opened again. His tongue crept out to his lower lip as his fingers danced across the keyboard. Clickety click. "She has a website."

Right. Who needed the yellow pages anymore? I snuggled closer to get a better look. Sure enough, Elizabeth Moser's website revealed her as Cadyville's newest and most innovative psychotherapist. Lots of testimonials attested to that, and Elizabeth herself went on and on about it. Yet there didn't seem to be any specifics regarding why she was considered — or considered herself to be — particularly innovative. Mostly, she just seemed new to the game.

Her face smiled out from the corner of the web page, sincere and helpful and surely no older than forty. Light brown hair streaked with blond and parted in the middle fell to her shoulders. Brown eyes. Freckles. A small gap between her front teeth.

"Looks like she works out of the old Blackwell house over on Sixth Street," he said. "Do you have a pen?"

Dutifully, I wrote down the phone number he recited. "First thing tomorrow I'll give her a call and get these back to her."

"Guess I'm out the four dollars." Actual regret in his voice.

"Buck up. I'll buy you some brand-new tapes for your little toy here."

"Mmmph."

I shrugged and rolled off the bed. "Maybe

31

I can find out whether she really considered this Swenson character to be a threat to someone." I slipped into a pair of sleeping shorts and a T-shirt.

"You're going to tell her you listened to the tapes." It wasn't a question.

"We'll see."

"She did sound like she planned to contact the department. Maybe it turned out to be a misunderstanding."

"Maybe. I'll be right back."

Down the hall, I washed my face and brushed my teeth. After listening to the tapes, I felt a kind of camaraderie with Elizabeth. That quake in her voice. She sounded so scared. What kind of misunderstanding created that kind of fear?

Back in the bedroom I crawled under the sheet and Barr turned out the light and wrapped his lanky form around me. Elizabeth Moser's voice followed me into my dreams.

At eight o'clock the next morning Erin was on her way to school, red notebook sticking out of her backpack, and Barr was tucking into a second helping of Dutch baby. I'd awakened with a sense of anticipation, knowing soon I'd be talking with Elizabeth Moser. I hoped she wouldn't be too upset that I'd listened to the tapes. Of course, it wasn't my fault she'd donated them to Granny's Attic.

In fact, I'd listened to *42R* several times that morning already. I transcribed the words while Barr was in the shower, even though I knew what she'd said by heart. I'd also checked the other unmarked tapes to see if there was anything on them. Just in case. But they were blank.

Glancing at the clock again, I asked Barr, "What time do you think she gets into the office?" I'd considered calling the number listed as her residence in the phone book but decided this was a professional matter.

He gave a one-shouldered shrug. "Try her now."

That was all I needed. I grabbed the phone and punched in the number.

"Blackwell Healing Center. How can I help you?"

"Elizabeth Moser, please."

Silence.

"Hello?"

"Yes, ma'am. I'm sorry, but Ms. Moser is no longer here."

"In the Blackwell Building?"

"Well, yes —"

"So she's moved?"

33

"Not exactly, ma'am. I'm afraid she's recently deceased."

FOUR

"Were you a client?" the receptionist asked.

"Um, no." My heart was pounding so hard I could hardly hear her. I'd been listening to a dead woman on those tapes. "Can you tell me how she died?" I finally managed to stammer out.

"It was a massive coronary."

"A heart attack?"

Barr put down his fork and watched me, the cold pancake in front of him forgotten.

"Yes, ma'am."

"When?"

"It was about a month ago."

I was so flummoxed I didn't know what else to ask. "Okay. Thank you." *Lame.* "Goodbye."

"Goodbye, ma'am."

"Wait!"

"Yes?"

"What's your name?"

"My name?"

35

"Yes. In case I have more questions."

"Bonnie Parr. I'm the receptionist for the four psychotherapists here."

"I see. Thank you again."

"You're welcome."

I hung up and sat down at the table. "You heard?"

"Elizabeth Moser is dead," Barr said.

"Uh-huh. Didn't she look a little young to have a heart attack? In that picture on her website?"

His shoulder rose and fell again — he looked utterly exhausted. "Maybe the picture isn't current."

"I wonder when she recorded those notes. And why she didn't contact the police like she said she was going to."

"Sophie Mae . . ."

"Seriously. Maybe she was going to talk to you guys and then had a heart attack and died before she could give you the heads-up on a possible murder."

"No."

"Barr —"

"Don't do this."

"Maybe she had a chance to warn the Swensons, though. I wonder how I could find out?"

He ran both palms over his face and sighed.

The phone rang. I got up and answered it, still distracted.

"What's wrong, Sophie Mae?" It was Erin's mother and our housemate, Meghan Bly.

"What? Oh, hi."

"You sound funny. Is Erin okay?"

"Oh, for heaven's sake. She's fine. Stop being such a worrywart, will you?" I heard the snap in my tone. "Sorry. I ran into a little snafu this morning, is all. Are you and Kelly having a good time?"

A pause as she no doubt considered whether to continue questioning me. She decided against it. "We're having a great time. It's crazy wonderful spending this much time together. And last night we went into New York for dinner, and he took me to Times Square. That's why I wasn't able to call until this morning."

"No problem." I grinned to myself. My best friend sounded almost giddy. I wished to heck Kelly would move out to Cadyville so they could really be together.

"What have you guys been up to?" she asked.

"Er . . ." Elizabeth Moser's tapes loomed large in my mind. I scrambled to come up with something else to talk about. "Um, my new helper starts this afternoon."

37

Meghan laughed. "You don't sound too sure about that."

"Oh, I'm sure. Her name is Penny, and now that her kids are off at college she wants to go back to work part-time. Give her something to do and some extra money."

Silence.

"Meghan?"

"I know all that, Sophie Mae. I was there when you hired her."

"Oh, well, of course you were. I guess I'm so excited to have some help that I forgot."

"Sophie Mae."

"Yes?"

"What's going on?"

"Nothing."

"Erin's a better liar than that."

"There's a lot happening right now, and I'm distracted with this new wholesale contract. Sorry if I repeated information you already knew, or if I seem flustered. I have to leave soon for Caladia Acres with a gift basket Tootie ordered. There's a lady there who's turning one hundred today."

"I'm sorry. Of course you're busy. I just wanted to check in. I'll call again tonight when Erin is there."

"Talk to you then. I'm glad you're having such a good time. Say 'hey' to Kelly from

Barr and me."

"Will do."

Punching off the cordless handset, I turned to find Barr watching me with an amused expression on his face.

"What?" I asked.

"You didn't tell her about the tapes."

I flipped my hand in the air. "Nothing to tell, at least not yet."

"At least not yet," he repeated.

"You are going to look into this, aren't you?" I asked. "Detectives have to follow-up on murder threats, right?"

"If there was one."

"You heard it!"

"That's not a murder threat. That's a psychotherapist making verbal notes about a patient."

"A patient who said he . . . she? . . . was going to kill someone. Same thing."

He shook his head. "It's not the same thing at all. It's hearsay. The tape could never be used as evidence."

I sank into a chair. "And Elizabeth Moser is dead, so she can't support it."

"Bingo."

"But what if someone gets hurt?"

"I'm sorry, hon. We're working on getting some serious bad guys right now. I'm way too busy to investigate the fantasies of a lunatic." He stood and stretched, his finger-tips brushing the ceiling. Then he stooped, and I tipped my head back so he could plant a nice big smacker on my lips. At least we weren't to the goodbye-peck-on-the-cheek stage of the marriage yet.

"How do you know it's a lunatic?" I hoped he wasn't referring to me.

"Because nobody in their right mind would tell a therapist they were going to kill someone. Elizabeth Moser must have decided the threat was empty, or she would have filed a report with us." He tossed the last words over his shoulder as he exited the kitchen, the box of tapes under his arm.

I followed him out to the front entryway. "Hey — are you actually taking those with you? What if someone's taken over her practice? What if they need her notes?"

He shrugged on a jacket. Looking at him still gave me a thrill. The way that one wavy lock of chestnut hair fell over his forehead, the way he moved, the cowboy boots and signature string ties. Today's was copper beaten into a cactus shape.

But good looking or not, he wasn't getting my point. Shaking off my oversexed distraction, I repeated, "What if she did take the threat seriously? What if she died before she had a chance to tell anyone?"

"That would be a bit convenient for someone, wouldn't it? Now I need you to let it drop," he said. "Those Swensons aren't to be trifled with. I'll see you tonight."

Jaw slack, I watched him stride down the front walk to his car. That rat! The Swensons weren't to be trifled with? How could he drop a hint like that and then walk away? After talking about the convenient death of a psychotherapist — which would benefit a possible murderer.

Hellllo? Mr. Police Detective, are you paying attention?

Okay, so he couldn't investigate something unofficial and based on hearsay to boot. His blasé attitude still struck me as odd. At least there was nothing to say I couldn't do a little digging around on my own. And I knew exactly where to start: Caladia Acres. If my favorite nonagenarian Tootie Hanover didn't have the lowdown on the Swenson family, one of her many friends would.

After all, I was already taking the Winding Road gift basket over to the nursing home anyway.

Right?

FIVE

"It's the third time we've had a one-hundredth birthday party this year," Tootie said, leaning heavily on her silver-headed cane. "God bless modern medicine."

We were slowly making our way around the large garden in back of Caladia Acres, stopping at each strategically placed bench for a quick sit-down. Two magnolias mirrored each other from opposite sides of the garden, their pinkish white, tulip-shaped flowers waving gently in the breeze. Delicate new leaves had unfurled from the maroon Japanese maples, and a Mexican orange looked ready to burst into bloom any second. Spent tulips waved abandoned yellow eyes, awaiting the gardener's knife. Bright indigo vinca crept beneath it all.

"Living to a hundred has never been all that unusual, has it?"

"A lot of people died from disease and accidents. But we had to work hard. I think the activity was healthier."

"Is that why you're walking more?"

She tipped her head forward. "That, and the yoga classes here seem to help as much as anything else. I stopped taking those arthritis pills they were giving me. More and more problems kept coming up on the news. Seems like anymore the cure is worse than the illness."

I wrinkled my forehead. "Not even pain pills?"

"Sometimes, when it's bad. Otherwise I couldn't get out of bed."

I winced. Sometimes the arthritis crippled Tootie to the degree that she used a wheelchair.

"So what's on your mind?" she asked, easing herself onto the next bench. She wore a crisp white shirt with beige slacks and a light blue cardigan to ward off the slight chill in the April morning air. Her white hair coiled in its usual patrician braid on top of her head, and intelligent brown eyes glided over the rhododendrons and azaleas just beginning to bloom. The breeze carried the sweet scent from the white blooms on the evergreen clematis. Everyone else was inside, getting ready for the party.

"Why do you think I have something on my mind?" I asked.

"Don't you?"

"Well . . ."

She smiled.

I rolled my eyes. "Okay, fine. Since you know everyone who has been around here for any amount of time, I thought you might be able to tell me about the Swenson clan."

She looked at me for a long moment. "Tell me why you want to know about them."

Darn it. But what did I expect from Tootie Hanover? So I told her about Barr finding the tapes at the thrift store and Erin listening to them.

"I wanted to know what she might have heard, so after I took them away from her, I listened to them, too. Turns out they're the verbal notes of a local psychotherapist."

Tootie looked alarmed.

"Don't worry. The therapist didn't use names. Except one — Swenson."

Speculation settled across Tootie's features as she put it together. "Don't you think you should return the tapes to the person who made them? They never should have left her office."

"I tried. She's dead."

Her eyes narrowed. "Dead."

"Heart attack, about a month ago."

"I see. So what is so interesting about the name Swenson? You are not typically a gossipy sort, so there must be something significant that's driving your inquiry."

I hesitated.

She waited.

I rubbed my face. "The therapist seemed worried about this person." My hands dropped to my lap, and our eyes met. "Apparently they said they were going to kill someone and make it look like an accident."

Tootie blinked.

"In her notes to herself, she didn't know whether to take them seriously or not." I raised my palms. "I don't either."

"Well. That is a quandary." Gripping her cane tightly, she prepared to push herself to her feet. "If I sit too long this chill will get into my bones."

I leapt up and cupped my hand under her other elbow to steady her. We continued on our slow circuit of the garden.

"The Swensons have been in this area for a long time. Dorothy is about five years younger than I am and still oversees the family business. She rules the whole lot of them — sometimes through intimidation, sometimes through fear, and always according to her idea of what's best for the family. At the same time, she's fiercely loyal to them all."

"But not exactly loving," I said.

"Love has different manifestations. She comes from an era where things were tough and families had to be strong in order to survive."

"So, how many family members are there?"

"Dorothy had one child, a son named Carl. He died more than thirty years ago, but he gave her four grandchildren first."

"How did he die?" I asked.

"Someone broke in. Carl had a gun, but the burglar took it away from him and shot him."

"Oh, wow. Killed with his own gun. Did they catch the guy who did it?"

"The very next day. Anyway, Carl Swenson was married to a very nice woman, but for some reason Dorothy never took to her daughter-in-law. She banned her from the family business, while enticing her grandchildren into it."

"Enticed? How?"

"Some force of will, though primarily with promises of big money when she dies."

Ooh. That sounded like motive. Maybe Dorothy was the intended victim. How very English manor house.

Tootie continued. "The daughter-in-law left town, remarried, and lives someplace in Virginia now."

"And the grandchildren?"

"All four still live in Cadyville."

"And they're all involved with Grendel Meadery."

"Indeed," she said. "Though in different capacities and to varying degrees. One of them owns the wine shop downtown."

"A Fine Body. I stop in once in a while to get wine for special occasions." Otherwise the grocery stores had pretty good selections of everyday grape. I wondered how a little town like Cadyville could keep a wine shop solvent.

"I read an article that said Grendel Meadery had gone international. Turned out that meant they expanded into Canada, but still. How long have they been in business?" I asked.

"Dorothy and her husband started making mead shortly after they were married, and it grew into a going concern. They might not be big all over the world, but Grendel ships all over the country."

"I've had their mead a few times. It's pretty good. I wonder how they make it."

Tootie smiled. "You do have an interest in the old ways, don't you? My folks made their own wine the whole time I was growing up, and then I did, too, for a while after I was married. We didn't use honey,

47

though."

"You made your own wine?"

"We made our own everything."

"Will you show me how?"

"Of course. It's the perfect time of year for dandelion wine. Be warned, though — you'll have to pick a lot of dandelions, because we'll only use the petals. And later in the summer I can show you how to make a lovely elderberry wine."

"I bet I can get Erin to help me pick the flowers."

"And I'll show her how to make ginger ale. It requires a little patience, but it's easy, and then she'll have something to drink, too."

"That's a good idea." I'd never thought about making dandelion wine, and I liked Tootie's comment about how her family made their own everything. I opened my mouth to ask more, then shut it again. Focus, Sophie Mae.

Tucking away my curiosity about wine making, I asked, "How old are the Swenson grandchildren?"

"Oh, older than you are, dear." She frowned. "At least I think so. The youngest one might be right about your age."

We'd passed one of the magnolia trees, and Tootie stopped at the bench across the garden from the one we'd sat on earlier. She eased her way onto it, and I settled in beside her. We watched the chickadees and nuthatches pick up seeds from the bird feeder and fly onto nearby branches to crack and eat them. Below the feeder, a half dozen spotted towhees pecked at the fallen bounty.

"Glen. Glenwood, actually," Tootie said.

"That's the youngest Swenson? He must be the one who owns A Fine Body. Is he good looking in a pretty kind of way? Dark hair, dark eyes, slight build?"

"That sounds like him." Tootie shifted, trying to find a bit of comfort on the hard bench.

"He's not so much with the mead making, then, other than carrying it in his store."

"Oh, I bet he knows his way around that meadery. Dorothy would have made sure of it."

"She sounds like a bit of a tyrant."

Tootie grimaced. "She . . . well, she knows what she wants and isn't afraid to go after it."

"What about the others?"

"The oldest of the lot is Victoria. She divorced her first husband and took back her maiden name. I believe she kept it when she remarried." Tootie looked into the distance. "She's in her late forties. I don't know what she does at the meadery, but I do remember several years ago I saw her at the Northwest Garden Show in the master gardener's booth."

"Does she seem like someone who would go to a therapist?"

"Oh, honey. I don't know her that well. I don't know any of them *that* well. Mostly I just know *of* them, if you know what I mean."

"I do."

She thought. "The next one in line is Quentin."

"The pharmacist."

"Yes. He works at Kringle's Drugs. Has for decades."

"I know his wife, Iris, through the artist's co-op. She's a wonderful quilter."

"She was ill a few years ago, wasn't she?" Tootie asked.

I nodded. "Cancer. But last I heard, the chemotherapy worked and she's still doing fine."

"Good." The word was decisive.

I agreed. I'd known too many people, including my first husband, who had succumbed to the disease. "So what's Quentin's connection to the meadery?"

"He's on the board of directors. Other than that, I don't know. His wife works there, though. She's a bookkeeper or accountant or some such." Tootie pushed herself back to her feet, and again I tried to help her without being obvious. She was a proud lady. "There was talk . . . well, that doesn't matter."

"Come on. Give."

"Sophie Mae, there is information, and there is gossip."

Fine time for her integrity to kick in. Though it had probably never kicked out.

"The last one is Willa. She's in her late thirties, just a few years older than Glenwood."

"And what 'information' can you give me about Willa?"

Tootie's eyes cut toward me, then returned to the path in front of her. "She works at Grendel, too. Something to do with keeping the production line going."

Pink spots high on her cheeks.

"And?" I couldn't help it. I'd rarely seen Tootie so discomfited.

A pause; then, "She prefers the . . . company . . . of women."

"So she's a lesbian?"

Tootie stopped and turned toward me, chin high, one hand on her hip while the other still held her cane. "Yes. She's a lesbian."

I tried not to smile. Cadyville was a provincial, largely white-bread town, and Tootie had lived here all her ninety-one years. "Do you have a problem with that?" I asked gently.

Her head jerked back a fraction of an inch, and she blinked. "Well, no. Not when you put it like that. It's probably a more sensible approach than some of the fool things girls and boys get up to."

I coughed and changed the subject. "How is it you know everyone in the family?"

"Oh, I don't. Of course, I've encountered each of them over the years, but I only really know Dorothy. In school she seemed so much younger than me, but when you get to be our age, five years is next to nothing."

I laughed.

Tootie held up one gnarled finger. "You should take into account that everything I'm telling you about Dorothy Swenson's grandchildren has been filtered through her. She comes up here to Caladia Acres regularly to visit her friends."

"Brings along that assistant of hers, too," called a voice from behind us. "Big woman, walks like she's got a stick up her butt."

I craned around to see Tootie's boyfriend, Felix, approaching. Though short and slight, he walked with long, swaggering steps, his

52

arms akimbo. He swooped in front of us and turned, eyes lighting up as they met Tootie's. He looked so much like a smitten leprechaun that I had to smile.

"Petunia, what are you doing out here? Everyone is getting ready for the festivities. I've got the limbo stick all ready to go."

Tootie directed a wry look his way. "Funny man."

"Petunia?" I asked. "I've never heard anyone call you that except Nurse Dunning."

"I don't like to call her Tootie," Felix said. "It sounds like a fart."

Sudden laughter boiled out of me, and I struggled to choke it back. Tootie, tall and elegant, smiled indulgently at her diminutive beau.

Love is such a strange thing.

Felix squeezed in between us and took Tootie's arm. "So what are you two doing out here? Laps?"

"Sophie Mae had some questions about Dorothy Swenson's family."

"Oh, Lord. Now what's Normal gotten up to?"

I moved in front of them, walking backwards as we made our way back toward the common room. Music and muted hoots of

53

laughter hinted at the party already starting within.

"Normal? Is that a name?"

Felix nodded. "An inaccurate one. Normal Brown is anything but normal."

"Do tell," I said. "And how's he related?"

Tootie frowned, but I ignored her. I was fine with a little gossip if Felix wanted to supply it.

"He's Dorothy's little brother. Four, five years younger'n her. Brown was her maiden name."

"So her 'little brother' is, like, eighty." I grinned.

"He's an evil old goat is what he is," Felix said. "Lives out north of town on a patch of land next to that Grendel Meadery place. See, he and his sister inherited all that land from their parents. They split it up between them. Dorothy and her husband started the meadery, but Normal subdivided part of his and built five or six houses to sell. Sure made his sister mad when he did that, but he's always been all about the money."

"Is he rich?"

"I doubt it. Just 'cause you make money don't mean you can keep it. But those houses? For a while he sold them, owner financed. But he'd only sell to people he knew couldn't afford the payments. So they'd put their money down and then last a year or two before missing a payment. He'd foreclose and turn around and sell the house again."

"Unfortunately, I don't think that's illegal," I said.

"It's not," Felix said. "But it sure made some people pretty mad. Some guy went after him with a gun awhile back, and he got wise. Stopped the scam and sold the houses outright. One of them grandkids bought one of them."

"Do you know which one?"

"Think it was the pharmacist. You know, ol' Normal used to be a 'shiner, too, but the market petered out. Rumor is he's up to something different these days."

"He made moonshine?"

"Oh, sure. Lots of us did. But he did it on a bigger scale, made real good money from it for a while, selling to the loggers in the fifties."

I stopped in front of the door. They stopped, too. "Are you saying you've had a little experience with the ol' white lightning yourself, Felix?"

His eyes flicked toward Tootie, and his grin fell away. "Well, not to speak of. Just helped my daddy some, is all."

She patted him on the arm. "Just as long

as I don't stumble on a still in the Caladia Acres pantry."

He brightened. "Anyways, now Normal's moved on from the 'shine."

"To what?"

"Er, well, I'm not sure I know. Just somethin' I heard, is all. Maybe he's got a nice marywanna grove back of his place."

The door opened and Ann Dunning, Tootie's favorite nurse, gestured us in. "We're getting ready to sing."

I held up my hand. "Thanks, but I've got to be going. You have fun."

Felix, now chatting with someone inside, held the door open for Tootie. She leaned toward me. "Call and update me on your quest."

"Do you think Dorothy Swenson will be here today?" I asked in a low voice.

"I don't know. Perhaps."

"Any chance you might ask her if any of her grandchildren are in therapy?"

She pressed her lips together. "I simply cannot imagine she'd share that information."

"You're probably right. Never mind." What was I thinking, asking her to do that? Sheesh.

Felix turned back to us.

I kissed Tootie on the cheek. "Thanks for

56

sharing your garden, and the information."

As I turned to go around to the front of the building where my Land Rover waited in the parking lot to ferry me to the next stop on my to-do list, Felix called from the doorway. "I don't know what you want with ol' Normal, but you be careful, Sophie Mae. And that Jakie is a mean one, too. Stay away from him."

Six

My Winding Road obligations called to me, but I couldn't resist taking a detour on the way back home. Slightly cloudy turned to completely overcast on the short drive from Caladia Acres to the Blackwell Building, and by the time I'd found parking on the street, a few scattered drops were spattering my windshield.

Who — or what — the heck was Jakie, I wondered as I hurried down the block. Felix made him sound like a badly behaved Rottweiler.

The Blackwell Building was a former residence, a large Victorian house on the edge of Cadyville's downtown historical district. The scrolls and gingerbread and curlicues boasted garish colors seemingly chosen for their unique ability to jar the senses and induce a mild feeling of nausea. Chartreuse warred with fuchsia and orange, bright against the gray sky.

Offices and workspaces filled the interior now. The only time I'd been there had been to pick up Barr from a meeting. I turned the knob, ducked in out of the rain, and paused to get my bearings. Teal and green paisley carpet stretched wall to wall in the entryway. It continued up the stairs on my left and spread down the short hallway ahead of me as well as the longer one to my right. The wooden sign on the wall listed a homeopath, a lawyer, a photographer, an accountant, and a nonprofit environmental group on the first floor. I turned toward the stairs and saw Elizabeth Moser listed, along with three other names and an arrow. All the other names were followed by various strings of letters, presumably indicating their vast qualifications. Elizabeth, however, had apparently dispensed with such hubris.

All the office doors on the first floor were closed. Classical music drifted through the tiny lobby. Straining, I detected the low murmur of voices from down the right-hand hallway. I was reluctant to disturb the air of quiet and found myself tiptoeing up the steps.

At the top of the stairs I rounded the corner into an expansive waiting area. An oversized mahogany desk dominated the back of the room. Five doors, all closed, marched around the perimeter of the space, four of them with nameplates mounted on them. An exit sign hung over the fifth. Fabric chairs that matched the dark green in the paisley carpet backed up against periwinkle walls. Magazines and boxes of tissue covered the side tables, and luxuriant palms reached out to an assortment of indefinite watercolor paintings in more greens and blues. A microwave, coffee maker, and ceramic cups sat on a table next to the water cooler. The room smelled like coffee and patchouli.

A large woman with spiked red — as in vermillion — hair sat behind the desk. She looked up, revealing a pleasant face unadorned by makeup. Quickly closing her *New Yorker,* she tucked it somewhere below the surface.

"Hello! Do you have an appointment?"

I recognized her voice.

"No, I'm afraid I don't." Now closer, I could see the silver stud in her left nostril. That couldn't help but be unsanitary. It looked nice with her earrings, though.

"Would you like to make one?" she asked.

"Thanks, but no. I'm here to talk to you, actually. It's Bonnie, right?"

Puzzlement replaced solicitousness. "Yes, that's me."

"We spoke earlier this morning, on the phone. About Elizabeth Moser?"

Her gaze cleared. "Oh, yes."

I approached the desk and placed my fingertips on it. "I have something that belonged to Dr. Moser. Can you tell me who has taken over her practice?"

"No one."

"No one?"

"I'm afraid Ms. Moser wasn't all that popular with her fellow therapists." Her hand swept out to indicate the doors that surrounded her.

"Everyone up here is a psychotherapist?" I asked.

She nodded. "Each has their own specialty." She pointed at the first door. "Trauma, PTSD, depression, and addiction." Then the next door. "Family counseling." Then, "Hypnosis and retrieval of blocked memories." And finally, "Body-mind therapy, our newest addition."

"Body-mind therapy?"

"Processing emotion that's stored at a cellular level."

I felt my eyebrows knot. "So what happened to Dr. Moser's clients?"

"Ms. Moser did not possess a doctorate. In fact, Ms. Moser did not possess a master's degree, and her BA was in interior design."

"I don't understand. How could she see patients then?"

"The state of Washington doesn't require psychotherapists to have any particular training. Of course, there are varying levels of certification, and most have an educational background to support their specialties, but anyone can hang out a shingle and purport to be a professional therapist."

"Ah. And that's what Elizabeth did."

She sniffed. "Indeed."

"And that's why her colleagues didn't care for her."

Bonnie gave a small nod of acquiescence.

Interesting. From those three tapes, I'd gleaned the flavor of how Elizabeth handled her clients and their problems. She sure seemed to know what she was doing as she dealt with a variety of situations. Degree or not, she'd struck me as both practical and professional. I wondered how much the others knew about how she worked. And I wondered which one, if any, she would ask for advice.

"Everyone seems to have a niche," I said. "What was Elizabeth's?"

"She didn't have one. She thought she could help everyone by listening and nodding. Told me once she was the kind of person other people like to talk to." Another sniff.

Not the most friendly work environment, if Bonnie was any indication. "So what happened to her clients after her death?"

"I contacted everyone on her client list to let them know what happened. Many asked for referrals, which I passed on to my doctors here to handle."

"Did some of them take on her clients?"

"Only a few of them continued with my doctors."

My doctors. Bonnie Parr sounded possessive yet maternal regarding the professionals she worked for.

She continued. "Some clients probably changed to other practitioners. And some may have dropped the idea of psychotherapy altogether."

"That seems unfortunate. So you know who all your doctors' clients are?"

A veil of discretion descended over her features. "I can't divulge that information."

"Oh, I understand. Believe me. But what if I told you that one of Ms. Moser's clients could be dangerous? Is there a protocol to deal with that?"

Her chin jerked up. "Dangerous? How so?"

"They threatened to kill someone."

"Oh." She waved her hand. "That's not unusual. People blurt out stuff like that all the time. It's kind of why they're here."

"To threaten others?"

"To get things off their chests."

Oh, for heaven's sake. What kind of thing was that to say?

Bonnie asked, "But how would you know about such a threat?"

I ran my hand through my hair. "It was on a tape."

Now she looked alarmed. "Of a client session?"

"No. Elizabeth's notes about her sessions. She said something about going to the police."

Bonnie Parr didn't look happy.

The door to my right opened then, and an older woman with stick-thin arms and weathered features darted out. "See you next week," she called over her shoulder, fumbling in her purse. As she brushed by me I saw a pack of cigarettes already in her hand. If I remembered correctly, that was the door behind which the hypnotist worked his magic.

"Dr. Simms, do you have a few minutes? This woman has a few questions about Elizabeth Moser," Bonnie said.

64

I stuck out my hand. "Sophie Mae Ambrose."

He shook it. "Garth Simms. Were you one of Elizabeth's clients?"

"No. I'd never even heard of her until I came across some of her recorded notes."

"Recorded notes?"

"Mini-cassettes we found at the thrift store."

One side of Simms' mouth rose in a half-grimace. "The tapes probably got mixed in with the other items they hauled over there. The landlord came in and cleared everything out of Moser's office two weeks back so the new tenant could move in soon."

"She wasn't married?"

He shook his head. "Getting over a nasty divorce. Wasn't even interested in dating yet — I know because I asked her out once."

So much for her coworkers disliking Elizabeth. I shot a glance at Bonnie's careful poker face.

Simms continued. "Her sister stopped by, but she didn't want to deal with Elizabeth's office. Said she had enough to deal with taking care of her house."

Charming. It sounded like Elizabeth Moser was quite alone in the world. It made her death all the more sad.

"Did she die at home?"

The expression on Bonnie's face indicated that perhaps I should show more decorum. I didn't care.

But Simms responded. "She did. The pizza delivery man found her."

I winced. Simms nodded his agreement.

Okay, time to regroup. "What happened to her other records?"

"When I contacted her clients, I told them to come pick up their files," Bonnie said. "Most did. Unfortunately, some were unable to."

"I'd think there would be enough personal information — sensitive personal information — in those files that people would climb all over themselves to retrieve them."

Simms half-sat on the edge of the desk and began flipping through a pile of mail.

His receptionist bobbed her head in agreement. "That's true, of course. But you see, there was a break-in. A box of hard-copy files was removed. So anyone whose information was in that box was out of luck."

A break-in? "Before or after her death?"

"Oh, right after."

Coincidence? Right . . .

"How many client files were in the box?"

Her chin rose. "A good half-dozen as I recall."

"They must have been furious," I

breathed.

"Oh, yes. Furious. Frantic. Embarrassed."

"Did you call the police?"

"Of course."

"Did the burglar take anything from the other offices?"

"No. We were very lucky. The police thought perhaps something had frightened him away."

I had a feeling it had less to do with luck than the fact that the intruder got exactly what he — or she — wanted and left.

Dr. Simms now watched me with interest. "You know Ms. Moser died from a heart attack, right? There was no foul play indicated."

"So I heard. Did she seem healthy?"

"She seemed like a hottie, if you want to know. Took good care of herself, jogged, the works."

But a heart attack wasn't suspicious?

"Were the files in alphabetical order?" Bonnie asked.

"They were."

"And which letters were missing?"

The receptionist looked the question at Simms, who looked at me. His head tipped forward a fraction, giving her permission to tell me.

"Q through S," she muttered.

Bingo.

"Do you still have her client list?" I asked.

She looked scandalized. "I can't show you that!"

"Can you tell me if one particular name is on it?"

"I don't think —"

Simms interrupted her. "What's the name?"

"Swenson," I blurted. The anticipation was killing me.

"Doctor —"

"She's already heard Elizabeth's notes. Take a look."

Looking grieved, Bonnie rooted around in a desk drawer. "Fine." She pulled out a file folder and opened it. Frowned down at it, then smiled up at me. "Sorry, Mrs. Ambrose. Nobody by that name on here."

I'd been hoping to learn the first name of the potential killer. I hadn't been prepared to be stopped in my tracks altogether. "I don't get it. That's the name Moser used when referring to the client who threatened murder."

"Hang on," Simms said. "What's this about murder?"

"Elizabeth had a client who threatened to kill someone. She was going to call the police and the client's family members. Elizabeth also said she was going to ask advice from a colleague. Did she mention anything about it to you, Doctor?"

He looked thoughtful. "No, she didn't. And if she'd talked to one of the others here about such a thing, I would have at least heard of it in a general way. We all confer together. Did she contact the police?"

I shook my head.

A quiet relief flooded his face. "Then she no doubt learned the threat was empty."

"Or she had a heart attack before she had a chance to tell anyone."

Simms and the receptionist looked at each other, and something passed between them. Finally he gave a kind of facial shrug, mostly eyebrows, and she turned back to me. "It's possible this Swenson could be one of her after-hours clients."

"After hours." That sounded downright sordid.

"She told us a few of her clients could only come at night. Because of jobs, family obligations, whatever. She wanted to be available to them." Bonnie pointed to the fifth door, the one with the Exit sign over it. "That's the back stairway. It's unlocked during the day, and some of our clients prefer to use it exclusively. In the evening the front and back doors are both locked, but the back door is equipped with a buzzer. That's how Elizabeth let her evening clients in and out."

I could tell Bonnie hadn't liked the arrangement. It went against her tendency toward control. Dr. Simms' bemused expression betrayed his own awareness of her disgruntlement.

"Are you saying Elizabeth Moser had clients you never met?" I asked.

A nod. "I felt it was quite unsafe, but she wouldn't listen."

"But they were just regular psychotherapy patients, right?"

Simms laughed. "I doubt Elizabeth was doing anything untoward."

Bonnie sniffed. "Who knows? I mean, now you're telling me one of these people might be a killer."

"Now, Bonnie," Dr. Simms said. "I'm sure it was just someone crying wolf."

Yeah. And we all knew how that worked out.

SEVEN

A royal blue PT Cruiser was parked in front of the house when I pulled up. The door opened and Penny Turner stepped to the street as soon as I turned off my engine. She smiled through maroon lipstick and waved at me, enthusiasm personified.

I got out of the Land Rover. "Sorry I'm late."

"No problem. I was here on time, though. Just so you know." In her mid-fifties, Penny had been looking for something to do after her two sons had graduated college and finally moved out of the house. I'd met her through a mutual friend, and when I mentioned that I was looking for a part-time helper, she jumped at the opportunity. I'd always had teenaged employees before, and while they'd worked out very well, I was looking forward to having someone a little older and wiser working for Winding Road. No doubt I'd be able to give her more responsibility, and her life experience would dictate a certain amount of common sense.

"Come on inside, and I'll show you where everything is and what we'll be doing."

Her wispy white-blond hair didn't budge despite her vigorous nod of agreement. Puffy appliqués of cats decorated her quilted cardigan. She smiled again, revealing large teeth. Her blue Bette Davis eyes crinkled deeply at the corners.

"I've really been looking forward to this. I've been so *bored* without my boys around."

"Well, I think we can do something about that. Plenty to do here." I unlocked the door and led her inside.

We had three hours before Erin came home from school. My seventeen-year-old helper, Cyan, would arrive shortly after that. That should be plenty of time to show Penny the ropes and set her to a task. Having good help would make all the difference to that delicate balance between my work and my marriage.

I made tea, and we took the cups down to my basement workroom. She paused upon entering, taking in the spacious room and the windows that lined the back wall to take advantage of the natural daylight. One end was outfitted with cupboards and shelving, with a stove and sink in the middle, and an industrial bread mixer I used to mix lye soap. The large island counter hunkered in front of them, close enough for convenience, far enough away for three or four people to move around comfortably. At the moment, the surface of the work area was covered with bath melts, still in their molds. I'd left them to cool overnight and hadn't had a chance to get back to them before I had to leave for Caladia Acres.

"I love the way it smells in here," Penny said.

"Me, too," I admitted. "It's one of the perks of the job. Lots of nice, relaxing aromas all around, all the time."

"Smells like mint. And something else."

"Peppermint, rosemary, eucalyptus, and tea tree oil. These are bath melts specially designed to ease colds, flu, or allergies."

"I'll have to try one. This time of year I get terrible allergies from the Scotch broom that grows along the highways. Now what's back there?" She pointed to my storeroom.

I waved her in. "This is where I keep the computer and printer. A lot of Winding Road business is conducted online. This is also how we create invoices, packing lists, orders, and keep track of inventory and supplies. But I'll continue to deal with all that for now."

No need to confuse the poor woman on her first day with a bunch of specialty programs and my own arcane system of spreadsheets. It would be nice to be able to offload some of that work down the road.

I gestured at the shelves lining the walls. "There you'll find raw ingredients like clays, butters, oatmeal, essential oils, colorants, and packaging materials. The cupboards in the main room contain bulk quantities of oils, salts, soap bases, and lye."

She looked alarmed. "Lye?"

"Well, yes. To make soap."

"I thought you just melted it and poured it into molds."

"That's exactly what you do for melt-and-pour. And we make some of that, using some unusual soap bases like emu, hemp, shea butter, and aloe vera. But I also make soap the old-fashioned way — using a few modern tools and standardized ingredients, of course — and that means combining lye with oils. The chemical reaction is called saponification."

"And it's safe?"

"The soap is, after it's cured, of course. In fact it's superior in many ways. The pH is lower than most commercial soaps, and it still contains the natural emollient glycerin. Most commercial processes eliminate that glycerin. The lye itself is quite dangerous, though. But don't worry. I'm the only one around here who works with it."

"Well, okay." Still doubtful, but she'd get used to the idea.

I gave her a light yellow chef's apron covered with stylized depictions of roosters to cover her clothes, then showed her how to take the bath melts out of the molds, package them in clear cellophane bags, and then tie on labels. As she got started I hovered for a while, watching. Finally she put down the mold she held and waved her hand at me.

"Sophie Mae, go on and do whatever you need to do. Don't you worry about me. I've raised two sons and a husband — I think I can handle this."

"You raised a husband?" I slid off the stool, taking her at her word. She was no kid, and I didn't need to monitor her every move.

"Honey, you don't know the half of it. You haven't been married long enough, but you'll find out."

I didn't mention that Barr was my second husband, or that my first one had died of lymphoma. We'd been together eight years, and I'd never felt like I had to mommy him.

"Okay, I'll leave you to it. Cyan will be

here in a few hours."

Penny sniffed. "That poor girl."

I paused. "Why do you say that?"

"I worry about both those girls. Because of their dad, and all."

Cyan's mom, Rhea, had introduced me to Penny. I hadn't received the impression they were terribly close, but maybe I was wrong.

"Their dad?"

Her nostrils flared. "He's having an affair."

"Oh, no. That's awful. What's Rhea going to do?"

She waved a label in the air. "Oh, she doesn't know about it."

Wait a minute. "Then how did you find out?"

"I was driving by and saw him go into a room at the Lucky 2 Motel." The look of gratification that crossed her face was truly disturbing.

"You do know he got laid off from Boeing, right? Now he's working for an electrician. Did he have his tools?" I asked.

She shrugged.

"Was he driving a company truck? Did you actually see a woman with him?"

"He was at the Lucky 2 Motel." Penny's big eyes bored into mine. "Poor Rhea. And those poor girls. Things like this can really

76

derail a teenaged girl, you know. Cause them to do things that would make you shudder."

Oh, for Pete's sake.

Unsettled, I went into the storeroom and spent the next two hours working on paperwork and updating my website. Occasionally I wandered out to check on Penny's progress. She was slow but steady, barely making it through half the melts in the time it would have taken me to pack up that bunch and another. But everything went slowly as you started, right? I had to give her time.

As I considered diving in to help, Cyan opened the basement door that led to the backyard and alley.

"You have perfect timing." I waved at the bath melts, cellophane bags, strings, and tags. "You know Penny, don't you?"

"Sure!" she said, shucking off her light jacket and donning her own brown-and-pink paisley apron.

And she knew the drill on Winding Road production, too. I left Penny's training in Cyan's younger but capable hands and went upstairs.

Sounds from Erin's room indicated she'd arrived home from school without my realizing it. I went down the hallway and

77

stopped in the doorway. She was changing into a pair of tennis shoes.

"What's up?" I asked.

"Taking eggs over to Bette. She asked for some when we had extra."

"Well, that's four dollars in your pocket."

She finished tying and stood. "If you guys would let me get a real flock, I could really make some money. Four hens don't lay enough."

"You know we aren't allowed to have more than four chickens inside the city limits."

"Well, that's just stupid."

I let that go without comment.

"You should come with me," Erin said.

"To Bette's? She only lives two blocks away. Take Brodie."

The little dog yipped at the mention of his name.

"I will. But then we could go downtown and get ice cream." She waggled her eyebrows like Groucho Marx, whom she'd probably never even heard of.

"You're really taking advantage of your mother being gone, aren't you?" Meghan was hell on junk food.

She grinned and nodded. "Wouldn't you be?"

I considered. The Cadyville Pie Shop made the best ice cream around. And it was three doors down from A Fine Body. Maybe I'd stop in and get a nice bottle of wine for dinner with Barr tonight.

"Deal," I said.

"Yay!"

Brodie wagged his tailless behind in approval.

"Go get his leash," I said, and headed upstairs to change my own shoes.

EIGHT

After dropping the eggs at our neighbor's, we walked the five blocks down to First Street, Cadyville's main drag. Ice cream came first: peach for Erin, chocolate-peanut butter for me, and a small dish of vanilla for Brodie. We found a bench overlooking the water and licked and slurped at our cones while watching three cormorants march up and down a cedar log lodged in the spring-swollen river. Then, wiping sticky fingers on paper napkins, we made our way back up the wooden steps to street level and began walking.

"I'm going to duck in here. It'll just take me a minute," I said when we were in front of the wine shop.

Erin bent down and scratched behind her corgi's velvet ears. "Okay. I'll stay outside with Brodie."

Inside the doorway, I paused. Off to the right, a huge display from Grendel Meadery took up a quarter of the space. Beyond, rows and rows of bottles marched down cherrywood shelves just below eye level. Scripted signs hanging from the ceiling identified groups of specific grape varieties. Others indicated countries of origin, and another announced a collection of wines from local Washington state wineries. Frosted bulbs above spotlighted the signs and glinted off the many bottles. The effect was elegant and inviting at the same time.

From the direction of the cash register on my left, I heard, "Can I help you find anything?"

The speaker approached. I immediately recognized Glenwood Swenson from my previous forays into A Fine Body. Tootie was right — he was about my age. Also mouthwateringly good looking. His dark hair swept back to reveal a pronounced widow's peak dipping into the middle of his forehead. Sapphire blue eyes smiled at me from under dark, arching eyebrows, and an aquiline nose offset his full mouth. He wore jeans and a black T-shirt that echoed every muscle in his body.

I stumbled over my response. "J . . . just looking for something to drink." Duh, Sophie Mae. "Some wine to drink, I mean."

No kidding.

Glenwood must have been used to women turning into blithering idiots around him, because he smoothly stepped in. "Is this intended for a dinner or another occasion?"

"Dinner," I managed. Erin was watching me through the window.

"And what will be served?"

"Um." Quickly my mind flicked through the possibilities. "Dungeness crab soaked in pepper butter," I said. "And artichokes served with garlic aioli. Rhubarb tart for dessert."

His smile was brilliant, all blinding white teeth and delight. "Sounds absolutely wonderful. Are you the cook?"

I nodded.

He glanced down at my left hand. "Lucky guy, your husband."

I looked down, too. "Yeah."

Erin was now pressed up to the window, both hands shielding her eyes from the sun's glare against the glass. I tried to ignore her.

"Come with me," Glenwood said. He led me to the back of the store and selected a bottle of wine from the bins on the back wall. "This Chardonnay goes nicely with seafood and garlic. It's dry, but with a buttery undertone."

I caught a glimpse of the price tag. My swallow was audible. Holy cow. "Maybe something a little less expensive?" I tried not to squeak.

He considered me. "Have you thought about serving mead? There are so many kinds, and it pairs with food as well as wine or beer. And," he winked, "I happen to carry every kind of Grendel Mead. I have one in mind for your menu."

I followed him to the extensive mead display. The meadery's logo was simply the word "Grendel" in a dark purple, Old English font on a pale gold background. Above was a stylized version of Beowulf's monster. The bottles were all dark blue and had swing-tops with metal bales holding down the rubber gaskets, which gave them an artisan feel. Each was sealed with a clear shrink-wrap band just like the ones I used for my Winding Road oatmeal-milk bath.

Glenwood handed me one. "Sage blossom sparkling mead."

"Sage blossom? I thought mead was mead."

"Oh, no. There are many varieties. Sparkling like champagne, or still like wine. Sweet, dry, fruity, or spicy. Some are fermented with grapes and are called pyments. If you add apples, it's called a cyser. Mead flavored with other fruits are melomels, and if you use spices or herbs, then the mead is called a methaglin. A bracket, sometimes called a braggot, is made with malt and has a hint of hoppiness, like beer."

"Good heavens," I said, reeling from all the terms. "I had no idea."

He pointed to the bottle in my hand. "That's a methaglin, which Grendel specializes in. It's force-carbonated, so it's fizzy like champagne, but brewed with a relatively low amount of honey so it's dry. The sage blossoms give it a subtle depth, and we throw in a few oak cubes to round that out."

"So you're involved with Grendel Meadery?" I asked.

He nodded. "My whole family is."

"Always have been," said a voice from behind him.

Glenwood turned. A white-haired woman in a wheelchair had entered the shop through a rear doorway. The woman pushing her chair towered above us all, her black hair pulled back from a bottom-of-the-ocean pale face in a severe bun. Her bright, dark eyes reminded me of the crows that frequented our yard.

The older woman spoke again, and my attention jerked from her attendant back to her. "My husband and I started the meadery in the late 1950s. It's been a family business ever since." Her white pageboy framed green eyes like mine, set above a large nose and stern lips. Heavily powdered skin hung in crepe-like folds around her neck. She held her chin high, as if she was daring me to question her.

"You must be Dorothy Swenson, then."

"I am." The words were abrupt, but she looked gratified that I knew who she was. She motioned with her hand, and the tall woman pushed her chair farther into the shop, reaching behind her to close the door.

I stepped forward and held out my hand. "Sophie Mae Ambrose. It's very nice to meet you."

She nodded as if to say, "Of course it is." Her palm was cool, the skin papery.

I shook it gently. "That must have been quite an enterprise then. This was practically the Wild West. I imagine you had some educating to do among the locals."

She sniffed. "Still do. But we ship all over the place now, so the Philistines in this little town are irrelevant."

Yow.

Glenwood flushed. "Grandmother . . ."

She ignored him. "I'm calling a family meeting this evening. Eight o'clock."

Ooh, a family meeting. Wonder what that was all about? Could they be discussing the warning a psychotherapist named Moser had delivered to their family?

Then I mentally shook my head. Of course not. If Elizabeth had contacted them, it would have been a month ago at least. They wouldn't have a family meeting about it now.

Unless it was *another* family meeting about the same thing?

Stop it, Sophie Mae.

Glenwood looked an apology at me. "Excuse me for just a moment?"

"Of course."

Dorothy's attendant appeared unfazed by the whole exchange. Even bored by it. When I managed to catch her eye, she looked right through me.

I moved to a table of Chateau Ste. Michelle wines, pretending to be absorbed in a Riesling label while listening hard.

"I have a date," Glenwood protested in a low voice.

Surprise, surprise. I wondered whether he had a steady girlfriend or spread his charms around. Or both. With those looks he *had* to be a player.

"Reschedule it," Dorothy said.

"But —"

"I expect you to be there with everyone else. No excuses." I glanced over to see the fierce glare she directed at her grandson.

After a few beats he ducked his head. "All right. I'll be there." Resigned.

"Naturally."

The door behind them opened again, and another woman entered the shop. Her own widow's peak reflected a close family resemblance. This must be either Victoria or Willa. Given the streaks of white hair that outlined her face, my guess was the former. She wore a white peasant blouse over a long denim skirt and Birkenstocks. Their voices lowered when she joined the confab.

"Glenwood! Customer!" Dorothy barked the words out in a loud, imperious tone. I almost dropped a bottle of Merlot.

He scurried past me — also a customer, I wanted to point out — to a woman wearing heels and a lot of glitter at neck and earlobes. As he went by, he smiled uncertainly. Suddenly he didn't seem as good-looking as I had first thought.

Erin still stood by the window with Brodie at her feet. I could tell she was starting to get impatient.

I moved to a rack of Chilean wines very near Dorothy. "I've met your other grandson," I said, all casual as I examined a Carmenere. "Quentin? Over at the pharmacy."

The newcomer showed surprise that I had spoken to her grandmother. Dorothy looked irritated, but answered. "Yes. He chose another profession, but he's still on the board of directors."

"Mead making sounds like a fascinating enterprise." *Lame.*

The attendant turned black bird eyes on me.

"I'm Victoria Swenson," said the other woman. "You should come out to Grendel and take a tour."

I introduced myself. Another handshake, firm and with a smile this time.

Dorothy waved her hand in the air, dismissing the idea. For the first time the tall woman spoke, her mellifluous voice at odds with her severe appearance. "Tours are on Mondays, Tuesdays, and Wednesdays at one thirty and three o'clock."

"Bah," Dorothy said.

"Um, thank you," I said to the attendant. She nodded her acknowledgment.

"Dog! No!"

Why was I the only one who jumped at Dorothy's sharp words? Were they all just used to it? I turned to see Erin in the open doorway with Brodie straining toward me on his short leash.

"Be out in a second," I called. She retreated to the sidewalk.

Dorothy frowned and held up a bony

finger. "Dogs simply cannot be allowed in a store like this."

"Of course not," I said. Not that it was her store to dictate such things. Poor Glenwood.

She held my gaze for a moment then gave one decisive inclination of her chin. It rose again. "Cabot! Home!"

At least this time I didn't jump. Dorothy was a woman of few words, but those were primarily loud imperatives directed at those around her. I was half-relieved to see Cabot swivel the chair and push her charge through to the back of the store without another word. If Dorothy had remained much longer, I wouldn't have been surprised to hear her shout, "Buy! Leave!"

Victoria turned back to me after her grandmother's exit. "She's something, isn't she?"

A noncommittal smile seemed the best response.

"Grandmother despises the tours out at the meadery. Feels it gives our secrets away. But Glen does a good job, and we generally have quite a few people. Especially on the weekends."

"Glenwood gives the tours?"

"Either him or Willa, my sister. But they were his idea in the first place. Speaking of

89

the meadery, I need to get back. It was lovely meeting you."

"Likewise."

I watched as she left. Her walk was stilted, but familiar. She moved like Tootie. Victoria Swenson was in considerable physical pain. Was she in mental pain as well? Had she been Elizabeth's client? I eyed Glenwood as he finished with his well-to-do customer. Or perhaps it had been the baby of the family, the one Dorothy had no qualms about humiliating in public.

Outside, Erin sat on the curb writing madly in her red notebook. Brodie lay beside her, chin on paws, brown eyes rolled up to watch passersby.

I hurried to the register with the bottle of sage blossom mead Glenwood had suggested, as well as an orange blossom mead that promised to be "brut dry."

"Your grandmother seems like a strong woman. Does she own part of the store?"

He wrapped the bottles in a paper bag and shoved it toward me. "No."

"And Cabot is her . . . ?"

"She's been mother's companion for over fifteen years."

"Hired companion?"

Glenwood took my proffered bill. "Well, she's not doing it out of the goodness of her heart. Luckily, she's also a nurse, so as Grandmother's health fails she can continue to look after her."

The prospect of his grandmother's failing health didn't seem to bother him that much.

"Thanks for all the advice," I said, all bright and cheery. "I'm really looking forward to trying out this mead."

"When you fall in love with it, you know where to find more." And there came that high-wattage smile again.

Hmm. I gave him a quick nod and went out to the sidewalk.

"What were you doing in there?" Erin asked as soon as we crossed First Street on our way home. "You said you'd only be a minute."

"Bought some honey wine for Barr and me. It's called mead. Sorry it took so long."

"You weren't just buying wine. I watched through the window. You talked to everyone in there."

"They're all part of the family that owns the Grendel Meadery. Have you heard of it?"

"I guess so."

"So I was asking them questions about how they do it."

"Is that your new thing? Making wine?"

The way she said it gave me pause. Perhaps Erin wasn't the only one who "developed enthusiasms" around our house.

"Maybe. Tootie said she'd show me how to make dandelion wine."

"Can I be there?"

"Only if you'll take notes."

She grinned. "Like you can stop me."

"Okay, then. We'll invite her and Felix over for dinner on Friday."

"I still think you were up to something in the wine store," Erin said.

Sheesh. She was like a dog gnawing on a bone.

"Does it have anything to do with the tapes?"

I stopped cold. "Why would you say that?"

"I heard you and Barr talking about the tapes. I'd really, really like to hear the rest of them."

I started walking again. "Too late. He's already taken them to work."

"So you're not investigating anything."

"Of course not."

"Because if you are, it would be a great subject for my book."

"Well, I'm afraid you're out of luck, then, Bug. Because there isn't an investigation for you to document. And if there were an investigation, it would be confidential and not your business."

"Sure."

That one word said it all.

NINE

I put the mead in the refrigerator to chill for dinner and went downstairs to check on my Winding Road workers. What I found was Cyan sitting alone at the work island, packaging bath melts like a mad woman.

"Where's Penny?"

"She had to leave."

"Leave? Why?"

Cyan shrugged. "Something about a family emergency. She said she'd be in tomorrow at the same time, though."

Oh, dear. A family emergency didn't sound good at all. "Well, let's hope everything is okay," I said.

"I'm almost finished here. I can stay another hour before I have to get home. Should I go ahead and start on the lip balm labels?"

I nodded automatically.

"I can probably get a lot done in an hour." She smiled her confidence at me.

"Thanks, Cyan. I appreciate it." But I was thinking that she shouldn't have to stay an hour more, that by now I'd expected the two of them together would be through with the bath melts and lip balm labels and onto putting shrink-wrap bands on the bottles of oatmeal-milk bath salts lined against the counter. If Cyan was just finishing up the bath melts now, Penny had been gone a long time.

"When did she leave?"

Cyan looked up. "Penny? About an hour ago."

She'd stayed longer than I thought. But then again, she was slow as molasses. I reminded myself she'd speed up as she got used to the work.

"There was a break-in at the dead psychotherapist's office," I announced when Barr walked in. I was preparing the artichokes to steam. The kitchen smelled of crushed garlic for the aioli. "They filed a police report, so you have it on record. The burglar stole all the 'S' files. It had to be a Swenson."

"Hello to you, too," he said, and kissed the back of my neck.

"Jeez, I'm sorry. Hi." I dried my hands on a kitchen towel and leaned back against him. "How was your day?"

95

He buried his face in my hair, and I heard him breathe in. "Frankly, it was pretty crappy. But now it's great."

I turned in his arms, and we spent a long moment getting reacquainted. After awhile, he began to pull away, but I drew him back. "I'm worried about you," I murmured in his ear.

"I'm fine."

"You're exhausted and more stressed than I've ever seen you. You aren't sleeping, and you're not eating well. There's something going on. I hate seeing you like this."

He smiled and kissed me again. "Thanks for worrying, but you don't have to. I'm working on something that will break soon. Very soon. In the meantime, I'll try not to let my work life spill into ours."

"I'm not complaining. And you don't have to protect me."

He opened his mouth to protest. I held up my hand. "I'm not asking for details, if you can't give them to me. But let me know if there's anything I can do. Deal?"

Inclining his head, he said "Deal" against my lips.

"Where's Erin?" he finally asked.

"She went to Zoe's horseback-riding lesson with her. She'll be home later."

"Is she going to want to take up riding now?"

"God, I hope not. It's an expensive sport," I said.

"But a lot of fun." Barr's family owned a guest ranch in Wyoming, and he'd grown up around horses. He'd even ridden in a few rodeos in his youth.

Releasing him, I said. "Erin's decided to write a book. Maybe she's doing research at the barn."

He snorted. "What kind of book?"

"Hmmm. Well, that's the thing. See, she's been snooping. I don't think she listened to all of Elizabeth's tapes, but she heard us talking." I paused. The only time we'd talked about the tapes when she was in the house had been when we were up in our apartment. The bedroom door hadn't been shut, though. I'd assumed she was asleep in her bedroom.

Why, that little stinker.

I continued. "So she thinks I'm investigating something on one of those tapes. Wants to write about it."

Silent, he filled the teakettle and fired up the burner under it. Settling himself at the table, he considered me. "Are you?"

"What? Investigating?"

"Yes."

It gave me pause, Barr asking the question straight out like that. I sank onto the chair across from him. "No one else seems to be."

"Sophie Mae, you seem obsessed by this therapist. There was never a report. There's been no violence, no complaint. Only a recording without enough specifics to do anything about, made by a woman who's dead. Like I said, it's hearsay at best."

"So someone has to die before you'll do anything?"

"My hands are tied. If I had all the time in the world, then maybe I could devote some of it to this. But nothing has happened so far, and it probably won't."

"But what if it *does?*" I insisted. "Wouldn't you feel terrible?"

He looked so tired. There were lines in his face that hadn't been there on our wedding day. My question seemed to deepen them.

"Yes. I'd feel terrible."

I got up and found the Earl Grey tea in the cupboard. "Well, then it won't hurt for me to ask around a little. I mean, wouldn't it be more important to save someone's life than to find their killer after they're dead?"

"You have to stay away from Normal Brown."

I put a cup with a teabag in front of him.

"Felix said something about him. He used to have a moonshine still or something, back in the woods."

"Or something is right. Ol' Normal has a long history with the department. He hangs with some rough folks. Really rough. I need you to stay away from him."

"What's he into?"

"It doesn't matter. I don't want you or Erin anywhere around the guy. Promise me."

I sat for a moment, absorbing that. "Okay. I promise. Do you think this Normal character is the one Elizabeth was talking about?"

Barr's lips twisted. "He's a gnarly old bastard. I'd have a hard time imagining him talking to a psychotherapist. And even if I'm wrong, and he did go against type, he's far too clever to talk out of school like that about killing someone. Normal's not your guy."

The teakettle began to whistle. I reached for it. "Doesn't sound like he's the potential killer. But if he's that nasty, it sure sounds like he'd be a good victim."

"Well then, you don't have to worry. Normal's managed to live into his eighties while tempting fate every day." He grimaced. "He appears to be bulletproof."

■ ■ ■ ■

The crab was delectable, the artichokes divine, and the mead went over very well indeed. Barr was skeptical at first, but he quickly converted.

"This is so crisp and dry. I expected something sweet and cloying," he said.

"Some are very sweet, like dessert wines. Glenwood Swenson recommended this for seafood."

His head jerked up at the name. I ignored him.

"Besides, the rhubarb tart will be, well, tart."

"Can I taste it?" Erin asked, reaching for my glass.

I moved it out of her reach. "No, you *may* not."

"Hey, I had to stand out on that sidewalk for, like, an hour while you bought it. Brodie even fell asleep. You could at least let me have some."

"Drink your root beer."

She blew a raspberry at me.

"Erin!"

Barr laughed. "You know, we used to make root beer when I was a kid."

"Really?" Erin drew the red notebook and

pencil out from where it had been laying on her lap.

Had she been taking notes the whole time we'd been eating?

I told myself to relax. We needed to watch what we said since the little pitcher had even bigger ears than normal lately, but we shouldn't interfere with the constant documentation of our lives. It would be over soon enough. Besides, if she was interested in writing down everything, then she wasn't focused on my inquiries alone.

"So how did you do it?" she asked, pencil poised.

"A couple of different ways. My grandma made it from scratch, but my mom used an extract. She only did it once, though. Because of the accident."

She scribbled, then paused. "What accident?"

Barr settled back in his chair and smiled. I felt a story coming on.

"Grandma used real roots — sarsaparilla, licorice, ginger, and wintergreen. I believe she added some vanilla bean, too. Sometimes she put some sassafras in, but that was harder to come by. She'd boil it all up and then add the 'tea' to a bunch of sugar dissolved in hot water. Used her big old canning kettle. Then she added yeast to that mixture. Lord, that stuff would boil and roil and foam for at least half a day, sometimes more. When it had settled down, we'd bottle it up and put caps on. Kept it down in the cellar where it was cool. It was my favorite thing to drink in the summer when I was a boy.

"When Mom decided to try it using root beer extract, Grandma thought that was cheating. But it came from the Hires company, and the way Mom saw it, they'd already done all the hard work of getting ahold of the roots and getting the flavor out of them. I daresay she was right."

Erin looked up from her notes again. "I thought you were going to tell me about an accident."

"Patience, Bug," I said.

She gave me a look.

Barr took a sip of mead. "It was the middle of the night —" Another sip. "— and suddenly we heard gunshots."

Erin's eyes grew big. Mine rolled toward the ceiling.

"Pop! Pop! Pop! It was loud, woke us all up. We ran downstairs and looked outside."

I opened my mouth. He shot me a warning glance. I shut my mouth and let him keep going.

"Pop! Pop! Pop! But it wasn't outside at

all. Someone was shooting *inside* the house."

He sat back and waited.

"Who?" she breathed.

"The shots were coming from the cellar. Dad and Randall and I started down the steps, careful and quiet. There was another shot, and we heard the sound of glass. I'll tell you, my mother grabbed us boys and pulled us back up fast as she could, calling to my dad, 'Vern, get up here! It's the root beer exploding.' " Erin looked confused.

"And that is exactly what it was. We stayed out of the way until all the bottles had broken. It took all the next day to clean up the sweet stickiness. And the house smelled like root beer for about a month. Kind of lost my taste for the stuff after that."

"The bottles exploded?" Erin asked. "Because your mom cheated?"

"Nah. Mom used the same method Grandma did, except for one thing."

"What was that?" I asked dutifully. My husband could sure draw things out.

"She didn't use the same yeast as her mother. And that made all the difference."

"Barr, did all that really happen?" I asked.

He looked offended. "Of course it did."

"Well, I've heard similar stories from everyone I've ever met who made their own root beer once upon a time. It always blows up in the basement, or the attic, or the barn. I sure hope nothing like that happens when we make dandelion wine."

"You're making dandelion wine?"

"Tootie's going to show us how. And Erin's going to help me pick the dandelions."

"I am?"

"You are."

My husband leaned back in his chair again, hands laced once more across his abdomen. "Did I ever tell you about when my grandmother decided to make dandelion wine? She —"

"Erin, come help me with the dishes," I said.

Barr laughed.

TEN

The tinkling of chimes announced my arrival as I opened the door to Kringle's Drugs the next day.

"Good morning, Sophie Mae." This from Warren Kringle himself, perched on a tall stool behind the register.

"How's it going, Warren? Business good?"

"Good enough. We had a run on Winding Road bath salts last week, and I could use some more of those lotion bars when you get a chance. Mother's Day coming up always depletes our reserves on the girly things."

Girly things. Right.

"I'll drop those items by as soon as I can," I assured him. "Right now I'm on a mission. Birthday card for Erin."

"Already? How old?"

"She'll be twelve in a week."

"Almost a teenager."

"And not about to let us forget it," I

called, walking away.

I made my way between the displays of gifts and knickknacks, stationery, wrapping paper, greeting cards, photo albums, and picture frames. The air smelled of spiced apple room spray, baby-powder sachets, and Pine-Sol. Near the back of the store a windowed counter accessed the small compounding pharmacy where Quentin Swenson mixed his potions and medications to order. The surrounding shelving units provided the usual over-the-counter drugstore fare.

A shuffle of papers, then the *pingpingping* of tablets dropping onto metal alerted me to the presence of someone in the rear of the pharmacy. I hoped it was Quentin, not his assistant, counting out pills.

Ducking down one short aisle, I perused the shelves for the cure to some innocuous ailment. Hmm. Unguents for athlete's foot? Naw. My gaze swept over cures for head lice, constipation, psoriasis, flatulence, and PMS. Ick. No way was I asking Quentin's advice about any of those. And I'd just look stupid if I inquired about something as boring as what brand of floss to use.

I paused in front of the weight-loss supplements. Not too yucky, and I wouldn't look too stupid. Only vain, and possibly fat. I could live with that. One bottle swore its contents would burn fat while you slept. Another offering was purportedly concocted of ancient African herbs. A third label boasted testimonials from an actress displaying her cut, tan, and oily abs.

Grabbing them all, I approached the back counter.

"Hello, Ms. Reynolds! What can I do for you today?" Quentin's voice boomed in the small space. His jowls quivered with delight. Even his comb-over looked delighted to see me.

"It's Ambrose now," I said. "Barr and I were married a few months back."

He slapped his palm to his forehead. "How could I have forgotten that? Unbelievable!"

"It's okay." His bouncy good humor was so infectious I couldn't help grinning. "Listen, I was wondering if you could steer me in the right direction." I spread the supplement packs on the counter. "Which of these is the most effective for quick weight loss?"

"Bah! What are you talking about?" The palm slap to the forehead again. "You don't need any of these. You are just perfect the way you are. Marriage obviously agrees with you."

I ducked my head, feigning embarrassment. "Thanks, Quentin. Still, bathing suit weather is right around the corner, and I've got an itty bitty bikini to fit into."

He waggled his eyebrows at me. "And will you be wearing that at the public pool? Because if you are, I might have to stop by for a look-see."

From most men that would sound smarmy; from Quentin it was just gentle teasing.

"Why, Mr. Swenson," I said in my best Southern belle. "You are a married man."

He laughed.

"How is Iris?" I asked. "I haven't run into her at the artist's co-op lately. I hope she's feeling well."

"She's doing great," he said. "Just been busy with her bookkeeping job."

"Out at the meadery?"

Here came that great big laugh again. "At least one of us is in my family's business."

He glanced down at the array of supplements on the counter, then leaned forward and slipped on the frameless half-glasses that hung on a lanyard around his neck. In a low voice, he said, "Do you really want to know about these products?"

I nodded.

"They're totally useless."

I blinked at his candor.

He continued. "If you're really worried, try to fit in a half-hour walk every day and cut back on pasta and potatoes."

"Practical advice." I leaned forward conspiratorially. "I wonder if you could give me some other advice."

He mirrored my posture, eyes wide, ready for the secret.

"I've got a friend who's new to town, and she's looking for a psychotherapist. I don't know what to tell her. You've lived here your whole life, and you're tapped into the medical community. Do you have any recommendations?"

Elbows on the counter, he stroked his chin. "A psychotherapist, you say."

I nodded. "Someone told her about a group that works out of the Blackwell Building."

"Hmmm." His thoughtful expression was a tad overblown. "This, um, 'friend' of yours . . ."

Uh-oh. Quentin thought I was making my friend up. That I needed a therapist. I opened my mouth to protest, but decided that would only make it worse. I'd learned a few things about effective fibbing over the last few years.

"What kind of therapy is she looking for?

Family-oriented? Cognitive behavioralism? Trauma recovery? Addiction, maybe, or marriage counseling?"

As he considered the sordid possibilities, a wicked gleam came into his eye. I could almost see his mind fill with a whole host of problems lurking behind the exterior of my seemingly ordinary life. The look reminded me a bit of Penny and the obvious delight she took in leaping to gossipy conclusions and then spreading them around.

"My friend — her name's Lucy — I don't know her all that well, so I'm not sure what kind of shrink she's in the market for. She was all set to go to one of the Blackwell therapists, but then the woman died suddenly from a heart attack. Morter, Miser. Something. So whatever she offered in the way of counseling is what my friend is looking for."

"Do you mean Elizabeth Moser?"

So he'd known her. It was a start.

I nodded enthusiastically. "That's her. Sad what happened. I hear she was pretty young."

But Quentin didn't look uncomfortable or even very interested. "Yes, quite unfortunate." He was looking over my shoulder. I glanced behind me. Mr. Kringle had abandoned the front counter and moved closer.

He stopped and fussed with a display of fountain pens.

"Did you know her?" I asked Quentin quickly.

An abbreviated shake of the head in the negative. "Not that well. Like you, she came in every once in awhile. I'm not sure what her therapeutic focus was. Your friend should check with Ms. Moser's colleagues to get a recommendation." Gone were the air quotes around the word "friend." Chalk one up for me.

But that was probably the best I'd get. If he was responsible for Elizabeth's death, or if he'd been one of her "S" clients, I wouldn't find out by talking with him more today.

"Thanks so much. I'll pass that on." I gathered the weight-loss supplements and returned them to their positions on the shelves. "Guess I'd better find that birthday card I came in for."

"You have a nice day, now, Mrs. Ambrose." And he turned toward the owner of the store who had moved up to the side of the counter.

I retreated to the card rack. After I'd found something suitable, I'd check out their fancy journals. Erin needed something nicer to write in than that red spiral notebook. Twelve years old. Good Lord, where had the time gone? Pretty soon she'd be driving.

What was that ticking sound? Not my biological clock, surely.

ELEVEN

Back home the garden needed — no, demanded — to be weeded. It was amazing how hard it was to keep up with everything when Meghan was gone. Maybe I'd grab Erin and get her to help me weed after she got home from school. In the meantime, I had an hour I could spare to the job myself. The chickens would be delighted with the gleanings, especially since once of the most common invaders among the early greens was chickweed — their favorite. It didn't make a bad salad for us humans, either, especially mixed in with some young dandelion greens.

The sun had burned off the clouds above, leaving only a few mares' tails wisping against the blue. It felt good on my bare arms and face. The dirt was damp but not soggy, perfect for pulling weeds from the raised beds.

I do some of my best thinking while working on mundane chores. Thoughts like: How do you find out if someone went to a therapist or not? And why hadn't Elizabeth contacted the police and the Swensons as soon as she was aware of the threat? Or had she contacted one or more of the family? Nothing about her name seemed to resonate with Quentin. Was I obsessing about something that was simply fiction? Had Elizabeth died from natural causes or not?

Okay, those were more questions than helpful thoughts.

Darn it, the buttercups were already invading the snap peas . . .

Focus.

So far I had a passing acquaintance with Quentin Swenson, and an even more passing one with Glenwood. The day before I'd met Dorothy and Victoria. That left Willa. Oh, and the mysterious Normal, Dorothy's brother. But Barr had warned me to stay away from him, and Felix had indicated in milder terms that Normal wasn't exactly one of the good guys.

Of course, I wasn't exactly looking for a good guy; I was looking for a murderer.

A murderer who went to a psychotherapist. That didn't sound like Normal. Besides, I'd promised.

For the life of me, I couldn't imagine Dorothy going to see Elizabeth. Even if I did manage to stretch my mind around that concept, there was no way she'd tell anyone if she was planning murder. I'd only met her once, but between that one encounter and what Tootie had told me, it was clear Dorothy would never have ceded control to anyone by giving them damning information.

In which case, Dorothy could be the potential victim. Now that was easy to imagine. Not only was she overbearing and difficult, but supposedly her death would net her relatives a significant amount of money.

What about Victoria? I didn't have a clear enough impression of her from the one meeting. I mentally added her to the list of real suspects, though she, of course, could also be a victim.

Then there was Glenwood. He was uber-aware of his own awesome looks, and came across all suave and smooth as silk — until Grandmother showed up and made him look like a fool. It had been half-embarrassing to see him reduced to a pathetic mouse in his own place of business by an old lady in a wheelchair. But wasn't that exactly the kind of person who went to a therapist on the sly? Someone who presented a strong (and handsome) face to the world yet needed someone to help him deal with all the secret insecurities and resentments?

I added Glenwood to the suspect list with his older sister. Which didn't remove him from the list of possible victims, of course.

Next was Quentin Swenson. Though I knew his wife better than I did him, Iris and I weren't exactly best friends. Of all the family I'd had the most interaction with Quentin, and he was the only one I'd actually talked to about Elizabeth Moser. His reaction to her death had been somewhat distant, but if he really had only known her to speak to that wasn't unusual. And my pointed questions about her age and psychotherapy specialty had met only ignorance.

Did I think he was lying? Not really. I tentatively took him off the suspect list forming in my brain and added him to the victim list. I could always add him back if new information came to light.

Victoria and Glenwood. That was all I had so far. I needed more information about them and about the other Swensons.

I leaned back on my haunches, gloved fingertips still trailing in the dirt of the asparagus bed. There was someone else I didn't know enough about. Elizabeth Moser herself. After all, she'd started this whole thing. And she could have ended it if she hadn't died. Her death — and the timing of it — was darned suspicious, and in the back of my mind looking into the Swenson family was not only to prevent a possible murder in the future, but trying to find out whether someone had killed Elizabeth.

Elizabeth, who had lived only a few blocks away.

Standing, I put my hands on my hips and surveyed the garden beds. I'd made some progress. They could keep for another day.

My watch told me I still had time for a little walk over to Avenue A.

I knew Elizabeth's address was in the phone book but went in the back door to the basement and looked it up online instead.

After I'd written it down, I brought up her psychotherapy website. My fingers brushed the screen over her gap-toothed smile for a moment before I shut the computer back down.

The postage-stamp lawn in front of Elizabeth's small white house desperately needed cutting. Maroon and white Oriental poppies grew up between blowsy pink peonies in the front garden, and some kind of fruit tree — peach? — shaded an ivied corner of the porch. A stone pathway led from the public sidewalk to the steps. The whole of the front yard was enclosed by a low wrought-iron fence. The overall effect was casual and welcoming.

Except for the closed curtains and neglected yard.

The metal gate felt cold in my hand. It squawked open and then closed behind me, and the stones wandered me up to the porch. Oh-so-casual, I looked around, wondering if any of the neighbors were watching. It wasn't like I was casing the joint, but they wouldn't know that. And in a town like Cadyville, folks would be paying attention to the empty house that belonged to the woman who died last month.

Or had it? She could very well have rented this house. By now it could be cleared out just like her office had been, and rented to someone else. The possibility made me inexplicably sad.

There was nothing to do but ring the bell, so I did.

Nothing.

I tried it again and again met with no response. The window in the upper third of the door reflected the sky. I stepped up and cupped my hands against the glass, peering inside. I could see all the way to the back of the house where a curtain was open. Plants clustered in front of that window, straining for sunlight. A wood-floored entryway opened into a living room. The built-in bookshelves were empty, and while there was a small table and a couple of floor lamps, I didn't see any larger furniture.

Backing up, I stepped off the porch and made my way under the fruit tree and around to the side of the house. I discovered two windows, both too tall for me to see over the sills, even on tiptoe. The first was curtained. The second showed a six-inch gap in the fabric, but I was still too short to see in very well. I looked around for something to stand on. An empty flowerpot caught my eye. I imagined Elizabeth filling it with dirt and artfully arranging annuals. The timbre of her voice echoed in my mind as I dragged it to the window, turned it over, and stepped up onto it.

A weathered pine dresser rested against the wall on the right. A vanity chair sat at an angle in the middle of the room. A Boston fern hung from the ceiling in one corner. There was no bed.

I saw all of that in the nanosecond my eye was drawn to the closet directly across from my perch. The open closet, with all the built-in shelves.

"What do you think you're doing? Get down from there this instant!"

My arms pinwheeled backward as I struggled not to fall on my behind. Staggering down from the upturned flowerpot, heart all thumpety-thump in my chest, I nearly knocked over the speaker.

She surveyed my antics with a less-than-amused turn to her nearly lipless mouth.

"Oh, you startled me," I rasped, then tried to clear my heart out of my throat. Tried again. "It's not what you think."

"And what, precisely, do I think?" Her short, iron-gray hair looked like it had been combed with a piece of buttered toast. Thick glasses cut some of the vitriol from the eyes behind them, but her gaze still pinned me to the ground.

"It looks bad, me looking in the house this way. But I only wanted to see if Elizabeth's things were still here."

The skin around those laser eyes relaxed the tiniest bit.

"See, I only heard of her death recently and . . ." I trailed off. Wait a minute. I really hadn't done anything wrong. Taking a step toward her, I asked, "Are you one of Elizabeth's neighbors?" Should I have used the

120

present tense? "Were you, I mean." That didn't sound right, either.

I shut up.

Her lips thinned even more. "I live next door. We keep an eye on each other around here."

"You know, I was just thinking that. It's one of the wonderful things about living in Cadyville. I'm Sophie Mae Ambrose."

"Mrs. Charles Deveaux."

Who introduced themselves with their husband's name anymore? Still, I'd taken Barr's last name. The alternative, of course, had been to keep my first husband's last name, and that just hadn't seemed right.

She sniffed. "I don't think you should be back here."

"All right," keeping my tone conversational. I turned the flowerpot over and returned it to its original position and began walking toward the front of the house. Mrs. Deveaux had no choice but to follow me.

"Did Elizabeth own this house?" I asked.

Suspicion filled her gaze. "You don't know?"

"I only know she lived here."

"From reading the obituaries?" All sarcastic.

I stopped and put my hands on my hips. "Listen, I understand you found me looking in the windows of your deceased neighbor's house. I get how that looks suspicious. But do I really look like a thief?"

"I don't know. What does a thief look like?"

"Tell you what. How about if you call the Cadyville police? Have them come over. In fact, ask for Detective Ambrose." I wasn't proud of what I was doing, but I wasn't above doing it, either.

She blinked.

"Yes, Ambrose. He's my husband, and I'm sure he can set the record straight."

Indecision played across her face, then seemed to settle. "Elizabeth owned this house. Fixed it up nice and took good care of the yard. Good neighbors are like gold. Who knows who will move in now." Mrs. Deveaux did not give the impression of great optimism.

"Who is taking care of her estate?" I asked.

"Her sister has been coming up from Yakima on the weekends, getting the house ready to sell, getting rid of Elizabeth's things. She didn't have a will, I guess. And she had a collection of craft supplies that her sister simply does not know what to do with. I told her to put it all on Craigslist."

I wanted to know so much more about Elizabeth. Dr. Simms didn't think she had a boyfriend or even dated. Did she have a best friend? How long had she lived here? Did she seem happy? But asking questions like that would only reveal I didn't really know her at all.

So I wrote down the name and phone number of the sister in Yakima, thanked Mrs. Charles Deveaux for her help, and encouraged her to continue keeping an eye on Elizabeth's little house.

As I walked home I thought about the questions I'd wanted to ask about Elizabeth. Barr was right; I kept thinking of the dead therapist as my friend, as someone who needed my help even though I'd never met her. Because of her practical problem solving. Because of her voice on the tapes.

Because of the fear I'd heard in that voice.

Those things, and the fact that an otherwise healthy person had died of a heart attack in her forties.

I really had a bad feeling about that last now. Because in Elizabeth's closet I had seen two very interesting things.

The first was shelves and shelves spilling over with balls and hanks and skeins of yarn. That told me she had been a knitter, weaver, or hooker — some kind of fiber artist. That would be the "collection" her cranky neighbor had mentioned. I knew exactly who would be interested in that stash, though. My friend and spinning mentor, Ruth Black. And it was quite likely Ruth could tell me more about Elizabeth as well. Knitters tend to socialize with each other.

The second thing I'd seen before being rudely interrupted was slightly more ominous. Tucked onto one of the fiber stash shelves were two bottles. Both had labels with the stylized Grendel design on them.

Elizabeth could have bought that mead. Anyone could have given it to her. It could be pure coincidence.

Sure.

TWELVE

I called Ruth Black to see if she knew Elizabeth Moser. She was running errands, but her Uncle Thaddeus assured me he'd give her the message when she got home.

"I'll be leaving shortly," I told him. "So maybe I'll try back later."

Erin walked in and started rooting through the refrigerator.

"What are you doing here?" I asked.

She looked at me like I was slow. "Teacher planning day. Early dismissal. Remember?"

"But I thought you were going over to Zoe's after school."

"Her mom is taking her shopping. I didn't want to go."

"Oh."

She sat down at the kitchen table with a glass of milk and a handful of molasses oatmeal cookies. "What's the big deal?"

Oh, to have that metabolism now. I nibbled at a pear and regretted skipping lunch. "Not a big deal. When we were at the wine shop yesterday, I found out they give tours at the Grendel Meadery. One starts in about half an hour, so I was going to take a quick buzz out there and see what's up. I can go another time, though."

Erin, mouth still full, stopped chewing and looked at me with pleading eyes. She swallowed and took a glug of milk. Through her white moustache she said, "I want to go with you."

"What on earth for?"

Her hand crept toward the red notebook on the table beside her glass. "Please?"

"You want to take notes about how to make mead?"

"Sure. Why do you really want to go on the tour?" she countered.

"To learn about how they make the honey wine. It's bound to be similar to what we'll be doing when your grandmother shows us how to make the dandelion wine."

She made a face.

"Remember Barr's root beer story?"

Her head bobbed and her eyes brightened at the reminder of exploding bottles.

"Well, Tootie said she'd show us how to make ginger beer, too."

"Ginger beer?"

"Ginger ale. Same thing."

126

"Oh! Okay."

"So you'll help me pick a big mess of dandelions on Friday this week? I need to call and make sure, but I imagine your Nana Tootie and Felix can come over for dinner."

"I still want to go to the meadery."

Erin sighed. So did I. And even though we'd left her alone at home for a few minutes here and there, I sure didn't want to do that with Meghan gone.

"I mean, you're not doing anything except going on a very, very interesting tour, right? It has nothing to do with those tapes, right? The ones you wouldn't let me listen to? The ones you *did* listen to?"

No one that young should have a smile that evil. She had me.

"Let me call and see if they'll let you come."

The girlish voice who answered the phone at the meadery assured me children could participate in the tour; they just couldn't sample any of the product in the tasting room.

Well, duh.

"Okay, Bug. You're in."

"Yay!" She wiped her mouth on her sleeve and jumped to her feet, notebook in hand.

Really? Well, okay.

Glimpses of the Grendel Meadery flashed through the tree trunks, afternoon sunlight reflecting off banks of high windows set into the brick façade. I steered the Land Rover onto the winding driveway and into the paved parking lot. At least a dozen vehicles clustered at the far end, near the door, and another dozen or so sat at the opposite end. The place was bigger than I'd thought. Pulling in next to a white Passat wagon, I noted a group of people standing by the door. They chatted and gestured with small glasses filled with what had to be mead, faces turned toward the golden light like flowers seeking solar nutrition.

Erin hopped out and stood with hands on hips. "Come on, Sophie Mae. We're going to miss it."

I dragged my tote bag out from behind the back seat and shut the door. "Relax. See all those people? I bet they're waiting to go on the tour, too."

Joining her, I ruffled her dark curls. She frowned up at me as we started walking. Glenwood Swenson opened the big glass door. He said something, and everyone began filing in. Erin grabbed my hand and tugged. "Come *on*."

We hurried and caught the door before it closed.

The lobby was large, with a glassed-in tasting room straight ahead. The roughened tongue-in-groove flooring, high beams overhead, and floor-to-ceiling windows provided a lodge-like feeling to the space. All it was missing was a moose head mounted on the wall. On the left a glass window exposed some of the meadery's actual working equipment. Framed placards and photographs related fun facts about mead, as well as a bit of history.

One said mead was the drink of love. Apparently the word "honeymoon" came from the practice of supplying newlyweds a month's worth of mead in the hope that it would aid in the conception of a child.

Fun fact, indeed.

Glenwood saw us and came over. "I had no idea I'd be honored with your presence so soon." He flashed a smile that didn't quite make it to his eyes.

Beside me, Erin scowled. I squeezed her shoulder.

"You made everything about mead sound so interesting," I said. "And the bottle we had list night with the crab and artichokes was delicious. I had to come and see how you make it."

A cough by my side. I squeezed again. Harder.

"I see you brought a friend." Glenwood kneeled in front of Erin and shoved his face up close to hers. "And how are you today?"

She leaned away. "Fine."

"Ah, I think I see." He nodded slowly like some ancient sage and stood.

"See what?" I asked.

"Mmm. You couldn't get a sitter, so your daughter had to come." Looked down his nose at her. "That's it, isn't it? Mom made you come, and you don't want to be here."

She bristled. I squeezed.

"Erin's my friend, and she really wanted to come."

He inclined his head. "Of course." Topped it off with a condescending smirk. "Well, enjoy."

"I'm sure we will," I called after him. So far I'd seen him sexy as hell, nice as pie, cowed as a bad puppy, and now downright obnoxious. Maybe he just wasn't any good with kids. Or maybe he was seriously schizophrenic.

"Sophie Mae?" Erin's voice was small. "Let go."

I stopped squeezing. "Sorry."

She craned her neck to look up at me.

"You don't *like* him, do you?"

I thought of his good looks, and how he'd made my stomach flutter before I met Barr. Funny: he didn't seem all that handsome now. "Not like, like. Just, you know, don't dislike. Mostly I can't figure him out."

"Well, I can. And he's icky."

Snort. "Get your notebook out."

There were seven people on the tour. Most were from out of town, or hosting guests from out of town. The entertainment options in Cadyville were limited, especially in the spring. Soon enough there would be Kla Ha Ya Days and the demolition derbies at the fairgrounds in Monroe, but the meadery tour was probably the closest thing we had to a cultural scene.

The group consisted of everything from an elderly gentleman nattily dressed for the golf course in argyle and touring cap, to Erin, wide-eyed and notebook at the ready. From the short, rotund guy with the loud mouth — "I'm an attorney, you know, a *litigator*" — to the willowy brunette who announced in painfully nasal tones that she "didn't drink anymore, I'm just here with my husband" about eighteen times before we even got started. But Glenwood zeroed in on a bright young thing in a yellow sundress. She couldn't have been more than

131

twenty-three or twenty-four, and she ate up his charm and looks like the bonbons they were.

Erin wrote it all down.

Glenwood gathered us all together in front of the glass wall. Behind him, stainless-steel tanks ranged among pipes and tubes and gauges. "First," he said. "We'll have a little history lesson."

Beside me, Erin sighed but scribbled away.

"Mead is the oldest alcoholic beverage in existence," Glenwood intoned.

"That's debatable," someone muttered. I looked around but couldn't identify the speaker.

Glenwood barreled on. "The theory is that it was discovered rather than invented. Paleolithic people came across a sweet, sticky substance in trees, made by bees. It became a food source, but happening upon it was rare, so they mixed it with plain water. Naturally occurring yeasts in the air occasionally fermented the honey-water mixture, creating a mood-elevating gift from the gods. They became better and better at creating the circumstances under which this 'gift' occurred, and the first brewers were born."

I leaned down and whispered, "Kind of like school, Bug?"

She shrugged.

Well, she was the one who'd insisted on coming with me.

"Nomads settled down and developed hive systems. The Romans and Greeks did the same." He went on to talk about the history of mead in Europe, of the references to mead in *Beowulf* that inspired the name of the Swenson meadery, the elite position of mead in the church and society when honey was rare, and the subsequent cycles of interest in the honey wine since then.

As someone who was naturally interested in all things handmade, normally I would have been hanging on his every word and struggling not to interrupt with questions. But something had caught my eye on the other side of the tanks and hoses: another glass wall. And that one appeared to open onto the garden of my dreams. Erin glanced up as I sidled to my left to get a better view.

The multitude of green — much of it made up of herbs I recognized even from the distance of three hundred feet or so — was interspersed with flowers and vines. From my vantage it appeared to be an enclosed brick courtyard. I wanted to ask why a meadery needed an elaborate garden like that. Perhaps it was simply for show.

Well, it was a show I was itching to get a

good look at.

I became aware of Glenwood speaking again. "When the Spaniards began conquering the New World, they brought fermentation practices with them. Colonial settlers fermented their own honey wine when sugar was scarce — and even when it wasn't."

In the garden, Victoria Swenson walked slowly past the far window.

"If you'll follow me, I'll show you how the magic begins." He grinned at the group, flirting with us as a whole while managing to give special attention to the sweetie in the sundress. He pushed the door open. One by one, we shuffled into the space we'd been looking at through the glass wall behind him, gathering in an attentive cluster.

The equipment surrounding us lent a cold quality to the room, all shiny and scientific. The painted concrete floor beneath us offset that, offering the impression of texture and warmth. It captured my imagination, and I was thinking of how to accomplish the same thing on the dull poured concrete of my workroom floor when Erin tugged at my arm and pointed.

She'd seen the garden, too.

With a sweeping gesture, Glenwood indicated a huge steel tank. "This is where we mix water and honey. First the water is heated to 180 degrees, and then the honey is introduced in this." He pointed to a smaller tank with holes in the sides. "It fits down inside and gradually the honey mixes with the hot water. The heat pasteurizes the mixture, killing the natural yeasts. Then we add specific yeast blends during the fermentation process. Since honey is a natural preservative, there is no need for the sulfates typically used in the production of fruit wines."

He continued talking about ratios and fermentation, focusing more and more on the young woman. Slowly, I stepped around to the floor-to-ceiling window that looked out upon the fifty-foot square patch of earth packed with luxuriant greenery. Erin shadowed my movements.

Glenwood's words faded from my attention as I approached the window and practically put my nose up against the glass. A quaint rock path wound between precise beds of luxuriant herbs interplanted with marigolds and nasturtiums. A garden hose curled near the wall, and drops of water glittered from the tips of leaves in the full sunlight. A two-foot-tall rosemary topiary boasted tiny blue flowers. Purple chive blossoms peeked out from beneath tansy. Fuzzy mullein squatted, ready to send up its tall yellow flower spike later in the season. And against the far wall towered what I was pretty sure was valerian.

Turning, I waited for Glenwood to pause in the tour monologue long enough for me to ask him about the garden. He led the group toward the bottling room, now rambling about the difference between fruit-infused nectars and forced carbonation. In the corner of the fermentation room, I spied a door that led outside and headed toward it.

"Come on, Bug."

THIRTEEN

Erin was right behind me. The door swung open at my touch, and we walked outside. I inhaled the intense combination of fragrant herbs.

Victoria Swenson approached from a shed on our left. Behind her, a woman followed on crutches, her left leg in a thick cast. Her short brunette hair revealed a peak over her forehead just like Glenwood's. Her facial features were so similar to his that they could have been twins, had she not been at least five years older than his thirty-five.

"This is wonderful." I held my arms out to encompass the courtyard. "We were on the tour, but when I saw this garden outside the window I couldn't resist."

Victoria frowned. "Well, this area isn't generally open to the public."

"But it's spectacular. Keeping it behind glass is simply too tantalizing. We can't be the only ones who have ventured out here."

"It's not on the tour."

Not exactly the response I'd been hoping for from a fellow gardener. I remembered what Tootie had told me about seeing Victoria in the master gardener's booth at the Northwest Garden Show in Seattle. So she wasn't a run-of-the-mill gardener.

"But I am glad you like it. It's my personal herb garden, though we use many of the things grown here to develop new flavors for Grendel methaglins. That's my sister's special skill, really." She indicated the woman on crutches. "This is Willa."

Willa Swenson did not smile, but when I walked up to her and stuck out my hand, she nodded pleasantly enough and leaned heavily on one crutch in order to grasp it. Her grip was firm, no-nonsense.

"I'm Sophie Mae Ambrose, and this is Erin."

Victoria pointed. "Right. From Glen's shop yesterday." She smiled at Erin. "Hello."

"Hi," she piped.

"Right," I said. "You mentioned the tours here at the meadery, and we wanted to come check it out. I'd never thought about how mead was made before, or all the different varieties available. We had some of your sage blossom mead the other night, and it was a big hit."

Willa looked pleased. "I'm very happy with the results of that experiment." Her voice was deep, warm.

"You seem to have been left behind," Victoria said. "Don't worry, another tour will start in about half an hour. You can go back to the tasting room and have something to drink while you wait."

What a nice way to try and kick us out. I looked around with regret, not wanting to leave. Erin wrote something in her notebook.

Willa's eyes cut to her sister and then back to us. "In the meantime perhaps you'd like to walk through and see a little more evidence of Vicky's green thumb at work out here."

I brightened. "I'd love to."

Something passed between the two sisters. Victoria turned to me and one side of her mouth turned up. "Can't deny a customer a tour now, can we?"

Slowly, to accommodate Willa's crutches and Victoria's painful gait, we walked down the main path that meandered through the center of the garden, examining the different plants. There were borage and milk thistle and feverfew, horehound and several varieties of sage, chervil and chamomile and calendula. Celery peeped out from under a

139

bush, and horseradish battled with mint for a final takeover of a back corner. Flowers backed up against the rear wall of the courtyard, along with belledonna and spires of foxglove.

"That's goji berry," Willa said, pointing to a small bush. "I bought some to eat and planted the seeds as a lark. It survived two years, so I guess it likes it here."

"Will you use it to flavor a mead?"

"I'll probably experiment with it."

Erin followed a few steps behind us, still scribbling furiously in her notebook. Was she making notes about the herbs? Or the people around her? She ignored me when I looked back. I shrugged and left her to it.

"I don't think I've ever seen oleander grown outside in this climate," I said.

"We bring that one inside during the winter months," Victoria explained.

"You have quite a few unusual herbs here. I know a bit about medicinal and aromatic plants, but several here I don't recognize." I indicated an innocuous sprig of green. "What's this?"

"That's black cohosh," Victoria said. "Good for balancing hormones and an effective nervine, but I use it to treat arthritis. See, I'm a master herbalist, so I do grow several varieties of plants that many gardeners haven't even heard about. I specialize in plants that can help with joint pain."

"My sister keeps her own arthritis under control with herbs and other natural measures, a considerable victory considering the pain she used to have to deal with," Willa said, fondness in her voice.

I glanced at Victoria, curious whether she was offended by her sister offering personal information to strangers.

But she seemed fine with it, nodding vigorously and pointing out bearberry, meadowsweet, yarrow, and bogbean. "And that's sarsaparilla." She pointed. "I dig it up and use the root."

"Like for root beer," I said, thinking of Barr's story.

"My grandmother has arthritis, too," Erin piped up. "It hurts a lot. Sometimes she uses a wheelchair."

Victoria stopped walking and looked down at Erin. "I'm very sorry to hear that. You know, I've developed a combination of herbs that I grow, dry, and then make into a tea. If you'd like to take some to your grandmother, I'll be happy to give you a sample. Then if she likes it, your mom here could buy some."

I said, "Erin is my friend's daughter, and her grandmother, Tootie, really her great-grandmother, is a good friend of mine. I'd like to take you up on your arthritis cure offer. I can only hope it will help her."

"Well, I don't know that I'd call it a cure. But it's helpful in reducing the pain and inflammation. I have some in the herb shed." She slowly turned back.

"Can I come with you?" Erin asked.

Victoria smiled down at her. "I'd be delighted." Together they returned to the shed.

"Are you a master herbalist as well?" I asked Willa.

She shook her head. "Naw. I mean, I know a fair amount about herbs, especially the ones that impart flavor. I like to experiment with creating new varieties of spiced and herbed methaglins." She pronounced it *ME-thu-glins.*

"Now, tell me again what those are, as opposed to mead or wine."

"Mead is honey wine. Methaglins are honey wine brewed with herbs and/or spices."

"So all methaglins are mead, but not all mead is a methaglin."

"Right. And then there are melomels, which is honey wine — mead — flavored with fruit."

"Sounds complicated."

"Not really." She shifted the crutches into a more comfortable position under her arms.

"That looks painful," I said, indicating the cast on Willa's lower leg.

She grimaced. "Itches like crazy. Cast'll be on for another three weeks. I don't know if I'll be able to stand it that long."

"Bad break?" I asked.

"Yeah. Kind of a freak accident."

"Here at the meadery?"

"Well, sort of. Several cases of mead fell on me in the warehouse. I'm sure someone simply stacked them in a hurry. We have an excellent safety record here," she assured me. "That kind of thing is very unusual, and not something that could endanger the public."

"Sounds like you'd definitely have to be in the wrong place at the wrong time."

My words seemed to convince her I didn't think Grendel was a dangerous place, but my mind was racing. That kind of accident could have done a lot more than break her leg. It could have killed her. So was it really an accident after all?

Willa leaned awkwardly forward and crushed a sage leaf between her fingers, brought it to her nose, and inhaled.

"Did you know a woman named Elizabeth Moser?" I asked, watching her closely.

Slowly, she shook her head, gazing into the air as she thought. "I don't think so." Then, more emphatically, "No, I don't know the name."

"She was a psychotherapist in town." Feeling my way, unsure of how much to reveal. If Willa was a victim, she wasn't the potential murderer. But I'd just met her, and maybe the accident at the meadery really was an accident. Should I show her all my cards? If she was the person Moser had spoken of, then would I be putting myself in danger? Or would the fact that someone knew about the threat neutralize the threatener?

"And . . . ?" She looked at me expectantly.

"And she's dead," I said. "Heart attack."

She waited, puzzlement on her face.

"In her notes, Moser mentioned one of her clients was named Swenson."

"I don't understand."

The door to the shed opened and Victoria emerged with a small jar in her hand. Erin followed, chattering away, red notebook momentarily forgotten.

I moved closer and put my hand on Willa's arm. "Do you know if any member of your family went to a psychotherapist?" My words were rushed.

Willa looked at me like I was the one who should have been seeing a therapist. "Isn't that kind of private?" She pulled her arm away from my grasp. "I'm not sure how that could be any of your business."

I mentally scrambled for an excuse to be asking impertinent questions of people I barely knew. Dang it, the only viable option appeared to be to come clean.

"In some notes I inadvertently came across, Elizabeth Moser said she was going to contact your family. She seemed to think one or more of you were in danger." Saying the words made me feel exposed, vulnerable.

"What kind of danger?" Willa asked.

"I don't know exactly. So she didn't contact you?"

She shook her head, the perfect picture of confusion.

"Well, I don't want to frighten you or anything. But you might want to let the rest of your family know."

"Know what?" Frustration leaked into her words. "That you came and told us some woman none of us has heard of thought we were in some kind of unspecified danger? I can just imagine how that would go over with Grandmother."

145

Victoria and Erin were nearly within ear-shot.

"I'd rather not talk about this in front of Erin, if that's okay. But I think you should tell the others in your family."

Willa frowned. "Yeah. Well, thanks for the heads-up."

There wasn't really anything else I could do. Maybe warning Willa would do some good in the long run. Maybe I'd done nothing but make a fool out of myself. Either of these sisters could have been Elizabeth Moser's client.

Erin skipped up to me, and a moment later Victoria handed me a half-pint jar filled with dried herbs. I held it up to the light, trying to identify the contents.

"Boiling water will release most of the medicinal qualities of the plants," she said. "But if your friend mulls wine with these herbs, the effect will be even greater."

"Wine? Really?"

"Wine is always best to extract the most from a combination of herbs, since some constituents are extractable by water and others are dissolved by alcohol."

Huh. The best combination of tea and tincture. Made sense.

"Well, thank you so much for your gener-osity," I said. "I'll let you know how it

146

works." I put my hand on Erin's shoulder, and we headed toward the door that led back inside the meadery. I opened the door and Erin went in.

Before following her inside, I turned back to Willa. "Are you sure those cases falling on you was really an accident, Willa?"

Her eyes widened. She began talking to Victoria as I let the door shut behind me.

FOURTEEN

"Sorry about that," I said. "Kind of derailed us from the tour, didn't I? But how 'bout that garden?"

"It's pretty." Erin said. "Victoria's nice. You should see all the stuff she's got in her shed."

Footsteps approached, and a man in a gray jumpsuit came in from the bottling room.

He pulled up short when he saw us. "Can I help you with something?"

"We got distracted and lost our tour," I explained. "Do you want to catch the next one?" I asked Erin.

She nodded enthusiastically. Then she whispered up at me, "But I have to use the restroom."

"There's one right off the lobby, where the next tour will start," Mr. Jumpsuit said.

Erin reddened. I thanked him, and we retraced our steps.

While Erin was in the restroom, I looked around the lobby, taking in details I hadn't had time to catch before we'd been whisked away on the tour.

In the tasting room, several people were already sampling different Grendel offerings. As I watched, Glenwood Swenson entered through a door set in the far wall with the other members of our tour group trailing behind him. Before they even got a chance to sit down they were given trays loaded with pre-poured samples.

I wandered over to look at the bold oil paintings that marched in a colorful row down a forest green wall opposite the glassed-in equipment room. The last picture was next to a short hallway that was almost invisible unless you were standing right in front of it. On the other side of the opening, a bushy schefflera blocked the view from the tasting room.

Glancing toward the closed restroom doors, I slipped around the corner. The forest green paint continued down the hallway walls, but the wooden floor of the lobby gave way to ugly, industrial carpeting that cushioned the sound of my footsteps.

"No!"

I nearly jumped out of my skin, but the word wasn't directed at me. It came from an open doorway spilling light into the hall from twenty feet away.

"I refuse to put you back into a position to threaten this family."

My ears perked up like Brodie's when there's bacon on the stove. The soft clank of metal on metal sounded from the open doorway, and I desperately looked around for someplace to hide. There was only one other door. I took a step and tried the knob. It was locked.

Well, of course it would be.

Breathing as quietly as I could, I just stood there.

"So stop asking. We have made other arrangements for shipping to Canada." Now I recognized Dorothy Swenson's voice.

"But darlin', you don't understand," a male voice whined. "*I* haven't been able to make other arrangements."

"Good. You need to stop that foolishness and simply stick to your other activities. Aren't they sketchy enough? I swear, Normal, I live in fear that someone will find out about all that nonsense. Do you even realize the position you could put this business in? Or do you simply not care?"

"Ah, Sis." More whine.

"Don't you 'ah, Sis' me, old man." Strident.

"Leave him be," snarled a new, deeper voice. "He should be the one running this outfit, anyway. He loaned you the seed money to start this place. And now you've got the nerve to tell us we can't be part of the Canada runs?"

"Please step away from the chair!" still another voice said. I was betting it was Cabot, Dorothy's nurse-companion.

Suddenly, the tallest man I'd ever seen strode into the hallway. A wizened gnome followed on his heels. A quick gasp from behind me, and I whirled to see Erin, notebook in hand, wide-eyed with fear.

"What are you doing down here?" the giant said. Every word sounded meaner than the last.

"We were, uh, looking for —"

Cabot wheeled Dorothy into the crowded space. "Private offices! You're not allowed. Return to the lobby. Now."

"— the restrooms," I finished. It was mildly believable.

The men came toward us. Erin squeaked and fled. I backed down the short hallway and into the lobby. When the big one ducked under the door lintel and into the light I almost gasped, too. He must have been well over seven feet, with translucently pale skin, dead blue eyes surrounded top and bottom by dark circles, and large-knuckled hands hanging like weights by his side.

He shambled past, glaring at me but not speaking. Several people in the tasting room were peering out at us now, either curious about what was going on or simply staring at Gigantor.

"They're right over there," the gnome said, pointing toward the restrooms. A wide smile split his face, deepening the multitude of wrinkles and corrugating his bald pate.

"Thank you." The words sounded a little shaky. "Come on." Hand on Erin's shoulder again, I steered her toward the ladies' room for a second visit.

So that was Normal Brown. And Jakie, the one Felix had warned me about, wasn't a mean dog after all. He was an enormous, scary person.

Erin didn't mind at all when I said we had to get home because Penny would be there soon.

"Cyan has to stay late at school this afternoon, so she won't be in until later," I said.

"I'll just plug away on my own, then," Penny said with great cheer.

Not so fast, new employee of mine. "I have plenty of work to do, too, so you won't be alone."

"Lovely! What shall I start with first?"

"I have a large order of lye soap that's finished curing and needs to be packaged." I led her into the storeroom and handed her a large basket. "I'll just fill this up with these cocoa butter bars and take them to the work island, where it'll be easier to spread out."

She peered with interest at the soap.

I grabbed a couple sheets of rice paper and a long ruler, along with a roll of printed labels, and laid them on top of the basket.

Out at the work island, I began unloading the soaps onto the clean surface. "These have been trimmed already, so try not to bump the edges on anything hard."

Penny held up one finger and waved it at me. "Don't you worry. I'll be handling this soap with kid gloves." She grinned. "Well, plastic, at least." She moved to her capacious quilted handbag, pulled out a pair of plastic gloves, and put them on. She snapped the wrist with a look of satisfaction.

"Gosh, that's not necessary," I said. "The soap will be fine if you simply wash your hands."

"I beg to differ. I'm sorry, dear, but I'm not getting any nasty lye on my skin."

Oh, brother. "The lye has been saponified

with the oil in the soap. It's not alkaline anymore."

"If you say so." She made no move to take off the gloves.

"Let me show you something." Back in the storeroom, I dug out a packet of pH papers. At the sink, I wet two of them. The first I dabbed against the opening of the dishwashing soap on the counter. It turned dark green: pH 8.5. The second strip I rubbed against one of the bars of cocoa butter soap ready for wrapping. It turned a light, yellowish green: pH 7.

Penny peered over my shoulder with great interest. "Ah."

"Exactly. This soap is far milder than the soap over there, and, in fact, milder than pretty much any over-the-counter commercial soap you buy."

She smiled at me.

Whatever. If she wanted to wear gloves whenever she worked with soap, I wouldn't stop her. Never mind that the latex was probably worse for her skin than the soap ever could be.

"Okay, if it makes you feel better," I said.

Still smiling, she took over unloading the soap in the basket onto the table.

I showed her how to tear the rice paper into strips by using the straight edge of the ruler. Then I tore those strips into shorter lengths to wrap around the bars of soap.

"Then fasten each with this Winding Road label."

Penny pointed at me. "You got it."

I left her to it and gathered olive oil, cocoa butter, and beeswax to make classic Winding Road lotion bars. I measured and weighed and poured, then set them to melting together over low heat. On one of the counters against the wall usually reserved for packing boxes I arranged rows of two-ounce molds shaped like leaves.

The beeswax was still melting, so I returned to the work island to give my helper a hand. Penny was still tearing the rice paper, ever so carefully, into precise strips.

"You can be a little sloppy. They're supposed to look torn."

She looked hurt.

I sighed internally and tore a few pieces by hand. Then wrap, sticker, wrap, sticker, wrap sticker, wrapsticker wrapsticker — bam bam bam. I was so used to having to hurry it didn't occur to me not to. It wasn't like I was trying to make her feel bad.

But she didn't seem to have noticed, still tearing the paper inch-by-careful-inch with latex-encased fingers.

Deliberately slowing my pace, I said,

"Cyan said you had to leave for a family emergency. I hope everything is okay."

Penny stopped what she was doing altogether, shaking her head. "That Robbie — he's my youngest, you know. Gets himself in the darndest situations."

"Oh?" I started ripping the rice paper into strips. One. Two.

"Do you know he ran out of gas? Must've ignored the fuel gauge."

Three. Four. "Was he out in the middle of nowhere?"

"Oh, no. Right downtown."

"Pretty close to the gas station," I said. Rip. Tear. Stack.

"Only two blocks away!"

"And he called you?"

She laughed, leaning forward on her elbows. I put the pile of rice paper in front of her, all ready to go around the soap.

"Can you believe it?"

What I couldn't believe was that she hadn't told him to hoof it down and get a gas can and some gas and let her get on with her work.

The corners of my mouth turned up. "Hmm." I could only hope that sounded more noncommittal than I felt.

I poured the lotion bars, put together some paperwork for my accountant, mixed

up two batches of Peppermint Sugar Glow
and cleaned up the "cooking" area.

Penny wrapped twenty-three bars of soap.

Sliding back onto the stool across from
her, I started wrapping and sticking again.
"Cyan will be here soon." Thank God.

"I do hope she's not in very much
trouble."

My forehead creased. "What do you
mean?"

"Having to stay after school and all."

"Oh, she's not in trouble. She's on the
prom committee, and they had a meeting,"
I said and rose. "I have some work to do on
the computer."

A heavy feeling in my gut, I went into the
storeroom. I'd lived thirty-seven years and
never had to fire anyone.

So far.

FIFTEEN

Footsteps clumping down the wooden stairs announced Cyan's arrival. "Erin let me in," she called to me. "Since Mom dropped me out front."

I came out of the storeroom. "No problem."

She shed her jacket and settled in at the table, immediately starting to label soap. She was almost as fast as I was. Rather than compete with her young co-worker, Penny seemed to slow down even more.

"Erin said you toured the Grendel Meadery today. I've never been out there," Cyan said.

"It was pretty interesting. You should go."

"The boys took me out there for Mother's Day last year," Penny said. "They have a little brunch. I got all loopy from that honey wine, and in the middle of the day, too!"

Cyan grinned. "I don't think they'll actually serve me any of it. Maybe I'll wait until

I'm legal to drink before doing the tour."

"That'll only be four years or so, right?"

Cyan stuck her tongue out at me.

"Those Swensons — the family that owns Grendel's? They're something else. Have you met any of them?" Penny asked.

"I'm pretty sure I've met all of them," I said. Suddenly Penny's propensity for gossip seemed less egregious.

"Of course, you know Quentin doesn't work out there. Had a bit of a falling out with his grandmother when he decided to pursue pharmaceuticals." The way she said it made him sound like a drug addict.

"I know Quentin. Saw him just today, over at Kringle's."

She shook her head and made a tsking sound. "So tragic."

"What is?" I asked reluctantly. Penny was probably going to talk about Quentin's wife's ordeal with cancer. Rumor mongering along those lines didn't sit well with me.

"The court case against him. About the little girl who died."

That got my attention. Got Cyan's as well. Oh, dear. "Could you go get more soap for us to wrap?" I asked her.

"You're kidding, right?"

"Huh-uh."

She rolled her eyes, slid off her stool, and

grabbed the basket. "Fine."

I turned back to Penny. "What girl?"

"Oh, Quentin didn't kill her — it was someone he was training who did it. Some kid going to community college over in Everett. Loaded the wrong pills into the prescription bottle. Poor little thing was dead the next day." Penny looked awfully happy as she related the tale. "Poof. Gone. Her parents were terribly upset."

No kidding.

"And Quentin felt just awful about it." Penny sat with her chin in her hands, apparently having abandoned the notion of wrapping soap altogether.

Cyan came back with a full basket of lavender-scented bars. "But it was an accident, right?"

"Sure it was. But the parents blame Quentin, so they've filed a civil suit against him. And they're working with the state legislature to create some new law that would make the training pharmacist liable for the mistakes of his charges. As if you can watch an employee all the time."

Hmmm. "Well, that is sad."

A veil of exaggerated concern fell across her features and she shook her head long and hard at the whole situation.

Given her willingness to jump to conclusions about Cyan's dad, who knew how much of the story about Quentin was true. At least it was something I could check out. But even then, how could it have any bearing on Elizabeth Moser and her belief there was a renegade Swenson?

Upstairs I found Erin in her bedroom, working away on her computer.

"Homework?" I asked.

She shook her head. "Typing up my notes from today."

"Erin." I moved into the room and sat on her bed.

The clickety clack of keys stopped, and she swiveled in her chair. "Don't tell me to stop. I'm not going to stop."

I held up my palms. "Stop what? Writing your book?"

"Following your investigation."

"Bug, there's nothing to investigate. After hearing the tape, we were worried that someone might be in danger. But the therapist never followed through and told anyone about her suspicions."

"That's because she died."

"Maybe," I conceded. "But see, now Barr knows, so the police have been informed even if it wasn't exactly through official channels. And the Swenson family knows now, too."

She frowned. "Did you tell that gardening lady today? When I was with Victoria?"

"Yes. She'll tell the rest of the family. Erin, we've done our due diligence. In fact, we've done more than we probably should have since none of this was ever our business to deal with in the first place." She opened her mouth to protest, but I kept speaking. "Now you can take whatever you want from your notes and write a story or make up a good ending, but any real-life investigating is over. Got it?"

"I guess." But she looked unconvinced. "The thing is, no one knows who the bad person is yet. Telling people there's a bad person isn't enough."

It seemed Erin knew everything I'd told Barr. Meghan was going to kill me.

"It'll have to be." I stood. "Someone in that family probably knows who Elizabeth Moser was talking about. They'll either deal with it among themselves, or will call the police."

Erin looked annoyed.

"And you can make up the rest of your book," I said. "It's fiction, right?"

"It's not about the book anymore! What if someone gets hurt? I wish Barr could do something. I mean, he's a real detective, with a real badge."

Leaning down, I gave her a big hug. "I know, honey. But his hands are tied. Nothing illegal has happened."

"That's a lousy answer," she mumbled against my shoulder.

I sighed. She was right.

The phone rang as I entered the kitchen. No doubt Meghan calling from New Jersey.

Great.

Grabbing up the receiver, I forced cheeriness into my "Hello!"

"Well, you do sound happy, Sophie Mae," was the dulcet reply.

Whew. Not Meghan. My mother.

"Hi, Anna Belle."

"Oh-ho, now you don't sound so happy. Who did you think was calling?"

"Meghan," I answered truthfully. "I'm afraid I'm really falling down on the job with Erin while she's gone."

"Oh, I'm sure that's not true. What happened?"

So I told my mother about the tapes, about Erin listening to them and wanting to write a book, and about how I had tried to control her exposure. About Barr's distraction and refusal to get involved. About the dead therapist, the Swensons, and the mead-ery.

"And now I've run into a big fat dead end. Splat."

She laughed. "You have had a busy couple of days, haven't you? But it sounds like you've done everything you could. And that clever girl of Meghan's — it's wonderful that she wants to write a book, for heaven's sake. She's growing up, and that involves pushing some boundaries. By allowing her to be involved a little bit, you've shown her that you respect and trust her. By limiting her participation and being up front about it, you're letting her know you're still in charge. I can't think Meghan would have handled the situation any better."

"Meghan wouldn't have been in this situation in the first place," I grumped. "She's blissfully immune to the forces that seem to draw me into these . . . investigations."

"Oh, poo. This could just have easily have happened to her. You're doing very well with Erin. You'll make a very good mother."

Wait. What?

Though the subject had certainly come up, I honestly didn't know whether Barr felt strongly about having children or not. I had to admit, the thought had crossed my mind a few times during the last week.

"Sophie Mae? Are you there?"

"I'm here."

"So when are you going to give your father and me a grandchild?"

"You did not just say that to me, did you? I mean, it's so cliché."

"Cliché schmliche. When are you getting pregnant?"

Oh, God. "Barr and I had a couple of conversations about having a baby early on, but they've fallen by the wayside."

She hesitated, then said, "Is everything all right with you two? You said something about him being distracted lately."

"I'm sure it's just work," I said.

Another pause. "You're still newlyweds. You have a whole long life ahead. But I can tell you right now that you need to tend to your marriage right from the beginning. Don't take anything for granted, and don't let anything — including work — drive a wedge between you. Distance can become a habit, and it's very hard to overcome once it's established."

"Sounds like you're speaking from experience."

"You know darn well I am. But things are different now, since you found out what happened to Bobby Lee."

The previous year I had traveled back to

Spring Creek, Colorado, to track down the truth about my brother's suicide.

"I'm glad," I said.

"In fact, the other night —"

"Sorry, Anna Belle. Gotta go."

Sixteen

After I narrowly escaped hearing about my parents' rekindled sex life, I made myself a cup of strong black tea with honey and settled at the kitchen table to think. Downstairs, Cyan was working late to make up for coming to work late, but Penny was long gone.

It had only been two days, but I already had a bad feeling about my new employee. She didn't show interest in her tasks or in learning more about handmade bath products. Rather, she seemed to view coming to work as a chance to get out of the house and socialize a bit. Also, it bothered me that on her very first day she'd been willing to up and leave to take her twenty-something son two blocks to a gas station. Either he was helpless to a spectacular degree, or she was willing to mommy him to the grave. Maybe both.

Even with the new contract, Winding

Road didn't make enough money that I could afford to keep an inefficient employee. Right now Cyan was finishing the job I'd expected Penny to complete, and the task I'd planned for her — filling jars with Peppermint Sugar Glow — would have to wait until the next day.

Erin's insistence that we should keep trying to figure out the threat to the Swenson family bothered me — partly because I agreed with her, and partly because I wanted her to drop it. The thing was, I understood why she didn't want to. It didn't help that I had no idea what else we could do.

At least my mother's encouraging words about how I'd handled Erin's involvement in the Swenson situation made me feel better. Maybe Meghan would see it the same way.

Maybe.

I took another sip of tea, relishing the tannic acid sliding down my throat.

Did I want to have a baby?

The thought was terrifying, yet full of exciting possibilities. And now that my mother had come right out and asked about it, I was going to worry at it like a sore tooth.

Thanks a lot, Anna Belle.

And what was going on with Barr? The

long work hours, his preoccupation at home, the disinterest in finding out who Elizabeth Moser was talking about on the tapes, even small changes in his eating habits. The night before I'd awakened to find him sitting up against the headboard, staring into the dark. When I asked what was wrong, he said it was nothing and then laid back down. I didn't think he'd gone right to sleep.

What was worrying him? Did it have to do with us? Me?

"Can I go over to Zoe's? Her mom's invited me for dinner." Erin stood in the doorway.

"I didn't hear the phone," I said.

She twiddled her fingers in front of her. "Ever hear of e-mail? You know, what I really need is my own cell phone. Then my friends and I can text."

"Tell it to your mom," I said. Total cop-out, but oh, well. "Is your homework done?"

"Yeah."

"Okay. Be back by eight."

She came into the kitchen and gave me a hug. It surprised me, since she had been backing off the hugs, and I'd just imposed one on her in her room.

"Thanks for letting me come to the meadery and take notes and stuff. It was fun."

I squeezed her back. "You're a strange kid, you know that?"

"Takes one to know one." She grinned and moved toward the front door. "Seeya." I heard it open, and then the latch snicked shut. Zoe lived in the next block, so at least Erin could walk.

And she'd be gone for dinner. Barr and I would be alone. Something romantic was in order. In my mind I ticked off what we had in the refrigerator. Eggs, of course. Always plenty of those. A chunk of gruyere cheese. Whipping cream. And in the backyard, the asparagus was ready for the first harvest, as were a variety of delicate salad greens. So: an asparagus and gruyere soufflé with a light salad, followed by dark chocolate mousse.

And rather than wine, mead — the drink of love. The sparkling orange blossom mead I'd picked up at A Fine Body promised to be dry and crisp. Perfect.

But first, a quick trip over to Caladia Acres to give Tootie the tea for her arthritis. I'd catch her up on the little I'd learned about Elizabeth and the Swenson family, and then buzz back home to make dinner and dig out the fancy china and candles.

I melted dark chocolate and whipped egg whites and then heavy cream. Strong coffee joined the chocolate, along with a good measure of Grand Marnier and a little vanilla. With slow care, I folded in the fluffy egg whites and cream, filled dessert dishes and set them in the fridge to chill.

Now for the garden produce. I had just grabbed a sharp knife and a basket when Barr came in the front door. I dropped everything and met him in the foyer, throwing my arms around him with a grin. "Hi."

He gave me a big smack on the lips. "Hi."

"Welcome home. Erin's gone to Zoe's, and I'm making us a romantic dinner."

He looked stricken. "Oh, no."

Crap. I dropped my arms and took a step back. " 'Oh, no' what?"

"I'm sorry, hon. I just dropped by to tell you I won't be home for dinner."

"Great. More paperwork?"

"No." Something in his tone.

I waited.

"Quentin Swenson is dead."

I opened my mouth. Shut my mouth. Opened it again. "What happened?"

"The paramedics say it looks like a heart attack, and the medical examiner is on her way. But given what we know about the possible threat to a Swenson, we're treating this as a homicide from the get-go."

I sagged against the wall. "Oh, Barr. I just

talked to him this morning, at Kringle's."

He looked alarmed. "What did you talk about?"

"I asked for a recommendation for a therapist, trying to find out whether he knew Elizabeth Moser."

Some of the alarm faded. "Could be worse. But dammit, Sophie Mae, I wish you'd stayed out of this."

"Hold it! There was no 'this' to stay out of. You said so yourself. Well, now you've got a dead body on your hands. I hope you're happy."

He didn't say anything. Just looked at me.

I sighed. "I'm sorry. I didn't mean it."

He walked over and kissed me on the forehead. "Yeah, you did. At least a little. And I don't blame you."

"No, I —"

"I have to go. Don't wait up."

The door shut quietly behind him. I stared at it for what seemed like a long time before I started to cry.

By the time Erin got home from Zoe's, all the Peppermint Sugar Glow was packaged and almost all of the chocolate mousse was gone.

"Did you guys have dessert?" I asked.

"Nah."

"Here. I saved you some." I thrust the last dessert dish at her.

She peered in the refrigerator. "Where's the rest?"

"I, um, ate it."

"All of it?"

"Yes, all of it," I snapped.

"Jeez, sorry." She looked at me more closely. "What's the matter?"

Oh, God. I didn't want to tell her. But she was going to find out. This was horrible.

"Bug, I've got some bad news."

"Somebody died, didn't they?" She breathed the words.

I nodded.

"Who?"

"Quentin Swenson. Looks like a heart attack."

She looked skeptical. "Like the therapist's?" She blew a raspberry. "Do you think it was a heart attack?"

Oh, how I hoped it was. "I don't know."

"Is that where Barr is?"

I nodded again. "He feels pretty awful."

"I bet." She seemed to be taking the news a lot better than I was. "Hey, don't feel bad. You were right. You did everything you could."

I fought back tears.

"Oh, Sophie Mae, don't cry." Her arms

173

went around me for the third time that day. "Were you guys friends or something?"

"Not really," I snuffled into the windbreaker she hadn't had a chance to take off yet. "I just knew him from the drugstore."

The phone rang. I turned to pick it up.

Erin shouldered me aside. "It's Mom. I'll take care of it."

With amazement and gratitude, I listened to my eleven, almost- twelve-year-old charge chat with her mother about the meadery tour, what she'd done over at Zoe's that evening, and how she was writing a book. They hadn't talked for a couple of days, and it was a long conversation.

At the end, Erin's eyes cut my way before she said, "She can't come to the phone right now. Do you want her to call you later?" She listened. "Okay. Talk to you tomorrow, then. I love you, too." And she hung up.

"There. Now you have some recovery time before you have to come clean with Mom and tell her what you've been up to."

"What we've been up to," I corrected.

"Yeah. That. Maybe you should leave me out."

I laughed. "Nice try."

SEVENTEEN

Barr didn't get home until almost two AM. He told me it looked like Quentin had died of heart failure, but what had caused it was still up in the air. There would be an autopsy and, because of Barr's suspicions, a full toxicology report. That would take a few days, though.

"If you find Quentin was poisoned, do you think you'll want to look at Elizabeth Moser's death again?" I asked. We were lying in bed in the dark.

"I already made inquiries. She was cremated. Short of a confession, there's little to investigate."

"Who found Quentin?"

Barr said, "His wife."

"Oh, no. Poor Iris."

"She came home from work and thought he was taking a nap on the sofa. When she couldn't rouse him for dinner, she discovered he'd died. But you'll be interested to know we found an open bottle of Grendel mead next to an empty glass on the coffee table. The lab techs will take a thorough look at it."

I propped up on one elbow and leaned over him. "I saw two bottles of Grendel mead in Elizabeth Moser's closet this morning."

A pause, then I heard my husband's carefully controlled voice. "What?"

"I know, I know. But I've felt all along that Elizabeth's death wasn't natural. Given what we heard on that tape — you still have the tapes, don't you?"

"Yes, dear. Tucked away safe and sound."

"Good. So anyway, her death was suspicious from the get-go, but I didn't know enough about her to be positive. So I went over to her house today. I found out her sister is taking care of her estate, and get this — Elizabeth has a fabulous stash of yarn in her closet."

He sighed. "You went in her house."

"Of course not. I looked in her window. The neighbor can verify that."

"Great."

"Barr, she had mead in there. You need to get a hold of it and test it along with Quentin's mead."

"I don't have enough probable cause to

get a warrant yet."

"Barr!"

I felt rather than saw the shrug. "Wait for the lab results on Quentin's mead. In the meantime, can we get a little shuteye?"

Lying back down, I stared hard at the night. "Penny told me something today about Quentin. Apparently there's a lawsuit against him because some girl died after receiving the wrong prescription. Did anyone tell you that tonight?"

My answer was a snore.

The next morning began with a severe caffeine deficit and didn't get much better. It hadn't been so easy for me to get to sleep after Barr had dropped off the night before. I kept wondering whether I should have warned Quentin directly about Elizabeth Moser's notes, rather than leaving it to his sisters. And I wanted to shake Barr awake and tell him about my trip to the meadery. But I figured he needed his sleep more than I needed to unburden myself.

He entered the kitchen looking more haggard than ever. Freshly showered, his brown eyes were red-rimmed from lack of sleep. His string tie — this one a hunk of polished turquoise — was slightly askew against his cream-colored shirt. I stood, still in bathrobe and ducky slippers, and adjusted it.

"Thanks." He ruffled my bed head and smiled.

"Breakfast is ready." I gestured vaguely toward the table.

Erin sat at the table, munching away and flipping through her social studies textbook.

"No time. Got to get to the cop shop."

I opened the cupboard and retrieved our biggest travel mug. I handed it to him and asked, "Was there really a civil case against Quentin? About a girl who died after taking the wrong medication?"

Erin didn't look up, but I knew she was listening.

Barr moved to the counter and poured coffee in the mug. "It came up when we questioned the Swensons last night. It wasn't a girl, though. A woman in her twenties. Name was Leed."

"Is that why you were so late? Interrogations?"

"Hardly. We asked a few questions — there was only time to cover the basics — but we'll follow-up with everyone again. Or rather, I will." He snapped the lid on the cup.

"Right."

His partner, Detective Robin Lane, had

no talent for questioning people, whether suspects or victims. She was abrasive and blunt, utterly without finesse. So whenever possible, Barr handled interviews. It put an extra load on him during investigations.

My tired husband refused my offer of a brown bag breakfast and left for the police station. The doorbell rang soon after, and Erin went to let her friend Zoe in. Unless one of them had to get there early or was running late, the two girls had walked to school together since the first grade.

"Hi, Sophie Mae," Zoe said, leaning against the kitchen doorjamb while Erin loaded her backpack in her bedroom.

"Hey," I managed.

"Are you sick?" she asked. She was a tall, gangly, athletic girl with mousy brown hair that she wore straight and tucked behind her ears. Orange sneakers peeped from beneath her purple jeans, and her T-shirt advertised some band I'd never heard of.

"Naw," Erin said from behind her. "She just doesn't like mornings."

I liked some mornings just fine, but I didn't have the energy to argue. "Have a good day at school."

"K!" they agreed in unison. Erin threw me a concerned look over her shoulder as they were leaving. I gave her a thumbs up to let her know I was okay.

I propped my chin on my hand and considered the platter of uneaten sausage, fruit, and toast in the middle of the butcher block table. Erin hadn't made much of a dent in it. I took a bite of the sausage. After watching the girls through the window for as long as he could see them, Brodie waddled in, laid down, and put his head on my foot.

I gave him the rest of the sausage.

Somehow I had to gather enough energy to face the day. I slurped coffee. Watched a slice of Granny Smith apple slowly turn brown.

Barr hadn't really answered my question about the civil suit against Quentin, but I didn't think it was intentional evasiveness. After all, he had a lot on his mind, and we were both tired as all get out.

The phone startled me out of my half trance. Brodie scrambled aside as I rose to answer it. I didn't recognize the caller ID.

"Mrs. Ambrose?"

"Yes."

"This is Willa Swenson."

Oh, dear. I took the phone back to the table and sat down. "Hello, Willa. I'm . . . I'm so sorry for your loss."

"So you know."

"Yes."

She sighed. "I suppose it's all over the news."

"I don't know whether it is or not. But my husband is a Cadyville police detective. He told me about Quentin yesterday."

"Oh. I must have met your husband last night. I take it he's not the stunning redhead?"

"No, that would be his partner."

"First they told Iris — that's Quentin's wife — that it was a heart attack. But then they asked a bunch of strange questions. Even mentioned murder. Do you know anything about that?"

I had to tread carefully. "I know they investigate all sudden deaths as possible homicides until that possibility is ruled out."

"So it has nothing to do with that therapist's notes you told me about?"

"Well . . ."

"That's what I thought. Why didn't the detectives bring up the notes when they were talking to us?" Willa asked.

"No idea." Because the evidence was hearsay? Because they wanted independent proof that a murder had been — or hadn't been — committed? Because a family member had just died?

"I want to know more," she said. "Can you meet with us?"

I waffled. I shouldn't. Barr wouldn't like it. "The police will fill you in. I'm sure of it."

"Yes, but you tried to warn us. We want to talk to you."

On the other hand, maybe I could find something out for him. Willa and I had hit it off well enough, and she sounded pretty reasonable on the phone.

"Please." She hesitated. "I might be able to help find out the truth."

Tricky. What if she'd killed Quentin?

"Do you have information that would help the police?"

"I . . . I'm not sure."

What if she hadn't killed Quentin?

"Where did you want to meet?" I asked.

"My house is in downtown Cadyville. My sister and brother and I will be here all morning." She gave me the address. It was easily walkable.

And unless they'd all done it, going over to her house seemed safe enough. Still, I had to make sure I wasn't stepping on anyone's toes.

"Let me make a phone call and get back to you." I glanced at the caller ID. "Can I call you at this number?"

She agreed. I hung up and called Barr's cell phone. It went straight to voicemail.

I waited for the tone. "It's me. Willa Swenson just called the house. She wants to know more about Elizabeth Moser's notes. Asked me to come over to her house and talk with her siblings. Call me back as soon as you can."

Darn it, what was I supposed to do now?

I made a decision. Take a shower, and wait for Barr to call back. But if he didn't get back to me in an hour, I'd go see what Willa had to say.

First I wanted to know more about that lawsuit against Quentin. I poured the last of the coffee into my mug and padded downstairs in my bathrobe. I sipped the lukewarm liquid while my computer revved up to speed. The empty spots on the storeroom shelves reminded me that I needed to do inventory and place some orders in the next day or so.

This was so not the best time for me to be running around town trying to find a hypothetical killer.

Or not so hypothetical.

And my new employee was more of a hindrance than a help.

I brought up the online archives for the *Cadyville Eye* again. It took longer to find what I was looking for than I'd anticipated, but finally I found the story from six years prior.

I should have remembered such a thing, but I'd only lived in Cadyville for a short time by then, and had been in mourning for my dead husband. I hadn't known any of the players in the Kringle's Drugs drama, so it hadn't penetrated my self-involvement at the time.

First off, Quentin hadn't given anyone the wrong prescription. And his pharmaceutical trainee hadn't put the wrong pills in the bottle either. But the victim — not a girl, as Penny had told me, but a woman in her twenties, as Barr said — suffered a severe allergic reaction to the medication that resulted in her death. Her name was Alison Leed. Unmarried, no children, but she had left behind two brothers and her parents.

They were the ones who had filed the civil lawsuit, first against the college student who had filled the prescription, then against Warren Kringle. In both of those cases, the cause of death was determined to be accidental. Sad, but no one's fault. And apparently Warren agreed, because he didn't fire his pharmacist.

But that was when the Leeds turned on Quentin. They cited negligence in his training practices and inadequate monitoring of his new assistant. And that wasn't the end of it. From what I could tell, the court case had dragged on for three years now and was fueling state legislation. The new law on the table would require felony prosecution for any pharmacist whose trainee made any mistake in dispensing prescription drugs.

I powered down my computer and took my empty cup back up to the kitchen. Could anyone in the dead girl's family have killed Quentin? Their concerted anger against him seemed like a good motive, but from the newspaper accounts they seemed more determined to channel their grief and fury into large-scale legal revenge.

Barr still hadn't called back. I tried him again. Didn't leave a message.

After showering, I cleaned up the kitchen, still waiting. A third call to his cell phone netted me voicemail once more.

"Okay, I'm going over there," I said into the phone. "Glenwood and Victoria will be there, too. I'll do my best to find out what I can without giving them too much information. That shouldn't be too hard, since I don't really have any." My laugh sounded forced because it was. On one hand, he'd asked me to help him investigate a murder the year before by just talking to the people involved. People who wouldn't be as likely to talk to him because he was the police. But I didn't know if he'd really be on board with this little trip.

Oh, well. I'd given him three chances to stop me.

I called Willa to let her know I was on my way over and donned a windbreaker with a hood over my fleece zip-up and jeans. Outside, gray clouds roiled like mercury overhead, but the rain held off. Fifteen minutes later I was standing on the sidewalk in front of Willa Swenson's tiny house.

EIGHTEEN

Painted sage green, Willa's house sat well back from Third Street. The lawn was precisely cut, the boxwood hedge freshly trimmed, the peach azaleas under the front windows bursting with color. The same white Passat wagon I'd parked next to at Grendel Meadery was parked in front. Leaning on her crutches, Willa opened the door when I was halfway up the sidewalk.

"Come on in."

"My husband knows I'm here."

She blinked, and the corners of her mouth turned up. "All right."

So what if I sounded paranoid. I didn't care. This woman could be a killer.

The front door opened directly into a small living room. Framed, black-and-white photographs of nature along with several pictures of Willa with another woman interrupted the cream walls. At least a dozen houseplants hung from the ceiling, reached up from large pots in the corners, or flourished on shelves among brightly colored book jackets. Vivid rag rugs were scattered seemingly at random across the floor planks. The wooden blinds were open but not pulled up, discouraging the dull daylight outside from entering. Instead, bright yellow light from two floor lamps illuminated the tableau.

Victoria perched on the chunky, rust-colored sofa, a cup and saucer next to an African violet on the glass table in front of her. Glenwood leaned against the cushions next to her, looking bored. And surprise, surprise: Dorothy Swenson sat across from them, Cabot beside her on a folding chair.

I had been invited to a Swenson family meeting.

"Hi," I said.

"Come in," Dorothy demanded.

Dishes clattered beyond the doorway set in the far wall, behind Dorothy. With a pang I wondered whether Normal was in attendance — and what Barr would have to say if he were.

Though frankly, I was way more worried about Jakie than Normal.

"We're having chamomile tea," Victoria said. "Would you like some?" Her puffy, red-rimmed eyes betrayed the grief her genteel words glossed over.

"No, thanks." I shrugged out of my windbreaker.

Willa took it from me and hung it on the heavily laden coat rack by the door. "Sit down, please." She gestured toward a pair of leather wingback chairs.

I dumped my tote bag under the coats and chose the empty chair nearest the door. The room felt small and stuffy with six people and a wheelchair in it. An open window would have done wonders.

A short woman with ginger-orange hair curled around her ears appeared in the doorway behind Dorothy. I recognized her from the photos on the walls. "I have to get to work now, at least for a little while. I'll be back as soon as I can get away."

Willa nodded. "Okay." The one word held a tremendous amount of weariness.

We heard the back door open and close as her girlfriend left the house.

Willa awkwardly sank into the other leather wingback and laid her crutches on the floor. She turned to me. "We'd like to know what those psychotherapist's notes said. Do you have a copy?"

On my walk over I'd thought about what to tell the Swensons about Elizabeth's notes, trying to figure out what Barr would do. I decided he'd play it close to the vest.

So now I shook my head. "I don't have a copy. The police have the tape."

"Tape?" Victoria's skepticism was evident.

So I related the story about the micro-cassette tapes and my attempts to return them. "But Elizabeth Moser had died of a heart attack, and there was no one to give them to."

"A heart attack?" Willa asked. "Like Quentin's?"

"I don't know the particulars, but yes. Which is why the police are looking extra carefully at your brother's death."

"And you gave these tapes to the police," Dorothy said.

"Well, my husband took them."

"The detective." Glenwood spoke for the first time.

"Right."

"Well, what did they say?" Dorothy pointed at me as if trying to push an *on* button.

"First, I'd like to know whether any of you knew Elizabeth Moser."

Willa shook her head. "I didn't. Vicky?"

Anger flashed in her sister's eyes. "Of course not."

Glenwood shook his head. "Nope."

Dorothy glared at me. "Do I look like

someone who would go to a psychotherapist?"

Beside her, Cabot smiled at the idea.

"No, ma'am," I admitted.

"Then what did she say?"

The actual transcription I'd made burned
a hole in my pocket, but I cleared my throat
and paraphrased. "That her client planned
to kill someone in the Swenson family and
make it look like an accident or natural
causes. Ms. Moser didn't know whether to
take the threat seriously or not, but she
planned to tell the police and your family,
just in case. She, um . . ."

"What?" Dorothy snapped.

"She implied that her client was also a
member of the Swenson family."

They all looked at each other with a
complicated combination of astonishment
and suspicion.

"Did she tell the cops?" Willa asked.

"No. Just like she didn't tell you, apparently. Now, was any other member of your
family in therapy?"

They all shook their heads.

"Normal, or Jakie?"

"Jakie's only our great uncle's lackey. He
isn't one of us," Glenwood said. No one
even entertained the notion that Normal
was in therapy.

"Is there anyone else I don't know about? Your mother?" I was curious whether that was a tender subject or not.

Dorothy's nostrils flared. The sisters exchanged a look. Victoria said, "Mother lives in Virginia with our stepfather. She hasn't been to the northwest in over four years, and she's certainly not one of this Moser woman's clients. And Daddy's been dead for years."

I'd been perched on the front of my chair. Now I settled against the back and looked over at Willa. "You mentioned on the phone that you might be able to help."

"Ridiculous!" Dorothy exclaimed.

A look passed between the sisters again. I wondered whether Glenwood ever felt left out, but he didn't even seem to notice. Victoria gave the tiniest shake of her head.

Willa turned back to me. "You're going to pass on anything we tell you to your husband, aren't you?"

"Are you saying you would rather I didn't? Because frankly, that doesn't make a lot of sense if you want the police to have all the information they need to investigate. In fact, I'm not sure why you're not telling the detectives in the first place."

Hesitation, then Willa seemed to make a decision. "First off, we wanted to know

192

more about what the therapist said. For all we knew, those notes you mentioned would tell us right away whether someone, you know . . . killed our brother."

Hard words to say. I knew from experience.

"So you had someone in mind already?"

Her face squinched in confusion, she examined the floor. "It didn't make sense. I mean, how could they do it?"

I waited.

Flicking a glance up at her grandmother, she continued. "Quentin had some trouble with a local family. The Leeds."

"Because of Alison Leed. The woman who died," I said.

Willa looked relieved, as did Victoria. Glenwood smirked. Dorothy pressed her lips together in irritation, and Cabot mirrored the gesture.

"So you already know," Willa said.

"And so do the police. You talked about it last night, didn't you?"

"We didn't. Iris might have."

"Well, the detectives know about the Leeds and the lawsuit. They'll look into it."

I, on the other hand, was much more interested in the bottles of mead found next to Quentin's body and in Elizabeth's closet. Who here knew about them?

193

Victoria said, "The Leed woman's death was a horrible tragedy, but it wasn't Quentin's fault."

"No charges filed." Dorothy sounded downright offended at the very notion that anyone would blame her grandson in any way. But Tootie had told me how loyal she was to her family.

"Not by the county attorney," I said. "But there were several civil cases, weren't there? In fact, the one against Quentin himself is still pending."

Glenwood weighed in. "Parents looking for someone to blame."

"Our brother wasn't responsible," Willa said. "They would have lost that case like they did the others. I'm sure of it."

They were all pretty loyal. What would a parent do if the law ignored their plea for justice? Would they take the law into their own hands, punish the person no one else would?

"What about the legislation —" My cell phone rang. "Excuse me." I rose and went outside, closing the front door behind me. "Hello?"

"Where are you?" Barr demanded.

"Um . . ."

"Are you at Willa Swenson's?"

"Er, yeah."

"I want you out of there right now."

"But —"

"Right now. This is an active investigation."

"Fine." I hung up.

A quick knock, and I re-entered the house. "I'm sorry, but I have to leave. Was there anything else you wanted to tell me before I go?"

Negative murmurs all around.

"Cabot! Home!"

The tall attendant immediately rose and moved around to the back of Dorothy's wheelchair. She pushed it toward me. "Could you open the door, please?"

I did, and the two sailed out to the front sidewalk. From there they turned left. I craned my head around the door. "Where are they going?"

"Grandmother lives a couple of blocks away," Willa said from behind me. I turned to see her adjusting her crutches and standing.

"Ms. Ambrose," Glenwood said, coming toward me.

I stepped out of the doorway to allow him through. He stopped, crowding my personal space. I could smell his breath. Peppermint and coffee.

"Thank you for indulging my sisters here.

I'm sure you're very busy. I look forward to seeing you the next time you're in the market for wine or mead."

"Goodbye." I watched him walk out to the late-model Mustang parked across the street. He didn't seem all that upset by his brother's death. Then again, everyone seemed to be keeping their emotions under tight control. A family trait, perhaps. Or else no one had really given a damn about Quentin.

Ducking back in, I reached for my windbreaker on the coat rack and accidentally knocked another jacket to the floor. Stooping to pick it up, I spied a large prescription bottle inside an open leather purse on the floor. I hung the jacket back up, put on my windbreaker, and stretched down for my tote, quickly reading the label on the bottle.

Interesting.

OxyContin. 30 mg dosage, prescribed to Victoria Swenson. With a big stylized K on the label, a la the Kringle's Drugs logo.

So much for controlling her arthritis pain with herbs.

Herbs. Methaglins were meads flavored with herbs. The garden at Grendel had poisonous herbs in it — both Willa and Victoria admitted they grew oleander and foxglove, which could be deadly. And Victoria had said wine was the best substance for herbal extractions.

Maybe I could salvage this trip after all.

I turned and found Victoria right behind me. "I'll walk out with you," she said.

"Listen, you two know a lot about herbs." I paused, then plunged in. "Is there one that would mimic a heart attack?"

Victoria wrapped a shawl around her shoulders and carefully bent to pick up the leather purse. "Digitalis would."

"Foxglove," I said. Whoop-de-do. I'd seen it in their garden, sure, but the trumpet-shaped flowers also grew in every field and ditch for miles around.

Willa said, "Nicotine."

Her sister nodded. "From nicotiana."

"I saw both of those in the herb garden at the meadery."

Victoria lifted one shoulder and let it drop. "Digitalis and nicotiana are pretty. We know enough not to brew with them."

Or enough *to* brew with them. I wanted another look at that herb garden. Who knew what other toxic goodies the Swenson sisters grew.

My cell phone rang again. I ignored it and moved toward the door. "I'm so sorry about your brother. Do you know when the service will be?"

Willa's brow wrinkled. "We can't arrange a date until they release his body."

Oh, God. I should have thought of that. She didn't seem the huggy type, so I patted her on the arm and said goodbye.

Out at the curb, her sister opened the door of the white Volkswagen.

"I gave my friend your tea last night," I said. "Already she swears it's helping her. Do you think I could get some more?"

"Sure. Come out to the meadery tomorrow. I'll be in the garden until noon or so. Plant therapy, you know."

"Of course. Thank you. I'll see you then." I pulled my phone out of my tote as I began hoofing it home.

NINETEEN

About a block away from Willa's, I called Barr back.

"Did you leave when I told you?" he asked. "Or just keep on asking questions?" No "Hi, Sweetie." Not even a hello.

"I tried calling you. Three times. I know you had your cell phone, and you chose not to answer it," I said.

"I was in the middle of working a case! I can't stop just because my wife calls."

"Well. Okay, I guess. But what's the big deal with my talking to Willa? After all, you said you wanted to talk with everyone again, and Robin won't be much help. As I recall, the last time there was a murder in Cadyville, you actually *asked* for my help. You wanted me to talk to people, gossip, get them to tell me things they wouldn't tell the police."

He sighed. "I know. And you did a great job. There's just something about this I don't like. It feels dangerous."

"Strangling someone wasn't dangerous?"

"Poison — if this is poison — is sneaky. It's a coward's weapon. Or a genius's. Cowards, especially smart ones, can be scary. And if this has to do with the notes on that tape, we're talking about someone who carefully plans ahead. I don't want anything to happen to you."

"If it makes you feel any better, those Swensons didn't tell me very much."

"You talked to both sisters and the brother?"

"As well as the grand dame herself, complete with creepy nurse attendant."

"And what did you learn?"

"Hypocrite."

"Yeah, yeah."

"Well, Dorothy Swenson thinks no one in her family can do any wrong. Willa knows her way around poisonous herbs, and Victoria is a master herbalist who grows plants like digitalis and nicotiana that can cause heart failure. I also happen to know from my visit to the meadery yesterday that they grow oleander and deadly nightshade, both of which are quite tox—"

"Wait a minute — you went to Grendel yesterday?" Barr interrupted.

"Erin and I took the tour. I wanted to tell

you all about it, but then Quentin went and died and you had to leave, and then you went to sleep before I could tell you, and then you left this morning without break —"

"Sophie Mae. Stop yelling."

A young man pushing a stroller on the other side of the street stared at me.

"Without breakfast." I said in a lower tone. "I'm sorry I haven't been around."

I waved my hand in the air as if Barr could see it. The guy across the street continued to gawk at my antics. With effort, I refrained from sticking my tongue out at him and yelling *boogada boogada boogada!*

"Do you want to hear this or not?" I couldn't help the impatience that oozed out around every word.

"Yes."

"Okay. So despite saying she doesn't use anything but herbs for her arthritis, Victoria has a big ol' bottle of OxyContin in her purse. From Kringle's."

A pause, then Barr said carefully. "Anything else?"

"Well, the Leed's lawsuit against Quentin came up, but they didn't add anything to it. And I did tell them all a little about Elizabeth Moser's tape, but just to see if anyone reacted."

"Did they?"

"Not one stinking bit."

He laughed. "Is that it?"

"Pretty much."

"Then I'll see you tonight. Try to stay out of trouble until then, okay? I love you."

"I love you, too." But I was talking to dead air.

When I got home, all I really wanted to do was take a nap. Unfortunately, that wasn't an option. I called Tootie and invited her and Felix over for dinner and wine making the next evening, and then headed down to the basement to get some work done.

Three batches of soap later, I was cleaning up the big industrial mixer when Penny knocked on the basement door.

"It's open," I called.

She came in, nose instantly wrinkling. "What smells?"

I laughed. "Everything. I was making soap earlier. Orangeclove, rosemary-peppermint, and lavender-basil."

"With lye?" Unbelievable that those wide eyes could get any wider.

"Now, don't you worry about it." I took her purse and set it out of the way in a cupboard. Handing her the yellow apron with the roosters on it, I gently steered her to the work island. "We have a whole new project to work on today."

She put the apron on over her pink, bead-studded sweatshirt and looked at me expectantly.

I'd decided that perhaps Penny needed a more hands-on management approach. After all, she'd been out of the workplace for a long time. It wasn't fair to expect her to jump in and take over like she was some kind of Sophie Mae clone.

"Have a seat. I have everything set up. See all these lotion bars?" They were stacked, already wrapped in cellophane, in a bin to her left.

She squinted at them.

"First, set out as many of these terra-cotta saucers as you can reach. Should be at least fifty. Then fill each with exactly this much excelsior." I demonstrated. "When they're all full, place a lotion bar gently on top. Then tie a length of ribbon around each one like this." I'd precut all the ribbon. "When you have all fifty, then unfold one of these boxes, put more excelsior on the bottom, put the lotion bar in its saucer on top, add a bit more excelsior so it doesn't move around during shipping, and close the box." I walked through each step. "Then stack the boxes five high at the other end of the counter."

"Oh, for heaven's sake," she said, settling her ample behind onto the stool. "It's not brain surgery."

"Of course not. Easy peasy. I need two gross of these to go out tomorrow."

There: clear goals, detailed instructions, time limit, and quantity desired.

"Two gross. That's, um . . ."

"Two hundred eighty-eight boxes, all told."

"And you want me to do all that in four hours?"

"Yes, please."

Throwing both hands up in the air, she said, "Well, all right then. I'll try."

I pressed my lips together and smiled. "That's all I can ask."

Inventory took another hour, and then I spent the next hour and a half on the phone and online, placing orders for bulk ingredients and packaging supplies. As I was getting ready to dive into processing four day's worth of retail orders from my website, the phone rang. The caller ID on the handset told me it was Meghan.

"Hey," I answered, heading toward the stairs. "Hang on a minute."

Penny barely spared me a quick glance as

she frantically dipped into the big bag of excelsior, lower lip held firmly between her teeth.

Once I was in the kitchen and the door to the basement was closed, I said, "Sorry about that."

"I caught you in the middle of something, didn't I?"

"That's okay. I wanted to get away from Penny to talk, though."

"Why?"

"She's kind of a gossip, likes to stick her nose in other people's business."

"You two should get along just fine, then."

"Shut up."

She laughed.

"Erin's not home yet," I said.

"That's okay. I kind of miss you, too, you know."

"Really?"

"Not as much as I thought I would, but yeah."

"Ha ha. Well, I really do miss you. How's Kelly?"

"How detailed an answer do you want?"

"Oh. Wow. Okay."

"I might have some good news when I get back," she said.

"Hmm. Sounds intriguing. Do tell."

"Not yet. Anyway, I wanted to check in

with you and see if everything's okay. Erin said you couldn't come to the phone last night. Were you just working?"

"Mmm-hmm." Great — my housemate's sixth sense for trouble was kicking in. "You just concentrate on having a good time in New Jersey. We'll have plenty of time to catch up when you get back on Saturday."

Brodie barked, and the front door opened and closed. I cast eyes skyward and thanked the timing gods.

"You're sure that —"

I cut her off. "Your offspring is now in the building. Do you want to talk to her?"

A moment's pause, then, "Put her on. But get ready to fill me in on everything that's been going on this week. And don't forget to set aside time on Sunday afternoon for Erin's birthday party."

"Don't worry. She's requested lemon cheesecake instead of cake, by the way."

"Naturally."

Erin walked into the kitchen.

"Here she is. Safe travels if I don't talk to you tomorrow." I handed the phone to Erin.

It wasn't that I was trying to keep my recent inquiries secret from my housemate, but there was no reason she should be distracted from her vacation time with Kelly.

At least that was what I told myself as I

went back downstairs.

Customer credit cards processed and packing slips printed, I went out to check on Penny. She looked fourteen different kinds of frazzled.

I put my hand on her shoulder. "It's okay. You can slow down a little." Though, truth be told, she had only managed to stack a hundred completed boxes.

"Where's Cyan?" Her usual good humor had evaporated.

"She's still working on the prom."

"She won't be in at all?"

"Later this evening, for a couple hours."

"But I can't stay that late!"

"I don't expect you to."

"In fact, my shift is over right now." She stood and took off her apron. "She'll just have to finish these up."

I looked at my watch. She'd put in her four hours all right. Pasting a smile on my face, I said, "See you tomorrow."

Suddenly Penny was all smiles again. "All righty — see you then."

Exhaustion swept over me, and my face dropped into my hands once she was out the door. Time to deal with the fact that she had to go. And soon.

TWENTY

After dinner, Erin finished up the history project she had due the next day, Barr worked on his laptop, and I spent the evening going through all the books we had that contained information about poisonous plants. It turned out we had quite a lot of information in our small gardening library. Many of the entries were warnings, since so many kinds of toxic greenery could be mistaken for beneficial herbs.

After a glorious eight hours of sleep, I made my second visit to Grendel Meadery on Friday morning. The tours wouldn't start until that afternoon, and the tasting room was empty except for two thirty-somethings staring all goo-goo eyed at each other over their mead samplers. From the lobby I eyed the hallway where Jakie had scared the living daylights out of me. It wasn't hard to resist the temptation to try my luck again.

Victoria had said she'd be in the herb garden. Looking around to see if anyone was watching, I made my way through the room full of tanks and hoses where Glenwood had pontificated on the history of honey and mead. I found the exterior door again easily. Pushing it open, I stepped out to the flagstone path and immediately inhaled the resinous aroma of the rosemary bush blooming by the window.

The chink of metal against terra-cotta sounded from the potting shed. The worn gray door was half closed. I eased farther into the blind spot it provided and walked quietly toward the back corner of the garden. There, spikes of foxglove leaned against the far wall of the courtyard, pale purple, apricot, and yellow. Used for heart conditions for centuries, digitalis was both poison and cure. Too much would result in a coronary — like the ones that killed Elizabeth Moser and Quentin Swenson. And there was nicotiana. Tobacco. Nicotine. Abused by smokers the world over in small doses but, again, an overdose would stop your heart. Who knew what else was in this garden? Death camas? Jimson weed?

I took out my cell phone and started snapping pictures. Bah. Foxglove and nicotiana were common garden flowers. I knew a lot about plants, but I was no master herbalist like Victoria. Maybe if I could compare some of these pictures to those in my books, I could identify all these plants. There were herbs and flowers galore, as well as medicinal foods. Purple puffs of aliums — chives, garlic, and onion — had just burst forth. I knew what they were but photographed them anyway. And near my feet, a few odd-looking celery plants thrived. No doubt there was a use for this mundane vegetable in traditional herbology.

The year before, we'd had trouble growing celery in our backyard garden, probably because of the shady spot where yours truly had tucked them into the ground. These were in full sunlight but had really skinny stems. Maybe it wasn't celery at all. Come to think of it, it almost looked like an exotic variety of parsley. I reached to pluck a leaf.

"Don't touch that."

Instantly feeling guilty, I jerked my hand back and straightened.

Willa stood outside the shed, crutches in one garden-gloved hand. Mud smeared the cast that reached up to her denim shorts, and water dappled her blue T-shirt. Sadness emanated from her posture. She looked about ten years older than she had the first time I'd met her in this garden.

When she recognized me her stony expression relaxed a little. "Sophie Mae. What are you doing out here?"

"Meeting Victoria. I need more of that tea for my friend's arthritis."

"Oh. Well, she's not here."

"Really?" I looked at my watch. "She knew I was coming. Said she'd be engaging in some garden therapy this morning."

Willa sighed. "I know. I'm not surprised, though. She's been forgetting a lot of things lately." She gestured toward the shed. "Her teas are in here, though. I'll get it for you."

"Okay. Thanks." I moved to stand in the open doorway. The shed, gray and dull on the outside, was full of scent and color inside. Cedar potting benches ran down either side of a narrow central aisle. Wide, shallow baskets of dried flowers covered the one on the right, while the opposite surface held flats of seedlings and terra-cotta pots. The earthy aroma of coffee-colored loam coiled up to meet the gentle perfume of lavender, eucalyptus, and mint bundles hanging from the ceiling.

"Do you know when your sister will be back?" I asked.

Willa pulled bottles and jars out of a cupboard at the back, squinting at the labels stuck on the front. "Probably over visiting

211

Iris, so who knows?"

"She's spending a lot of time over there? That's good. Poor Iris. This has been a hell of a year for her. I should stop by and see if there's anything I can do to help."

Willa looked over her shoulder. "You know her?"

"Only from the artists' co-op."

"Well, I'm sure she'd appreciate a visit. Their son is in the military overseas. He'll be home in another day or so, but until then Iris is staying in that house all by herself. I think she needs as much company as she can get." Willa seemed to find what she was looking for and carried the gallon jar over to the bench. "How much do you need?"

"I think a couple of ounces will be enough for now."

She measured out the herbal mixture into a bag on the scale. "Be sure to put this in a glass jar when you get home so the volatile oils don't evaporate."

"Don't worry. It's the same drill for the herbs I use in soap making." I paid Willa and we moved to the door.

"Willa! Line's down!" Dorothy barked from less than ten feet away.

Hand over my chest, I stopped dead in my tracks and tried to inhale. Who needed exotic herbs to induce a heart attack when

Dorothy Swenson could do it by yelling out of the blue?

Cabot loomed over the wheelchair like a sullen vulture. Her jet eyes flashed recognition when she saw me. I tried a smile.

Scooting past me on her crutches, Willa asked, "What's wrong?"

"The bottle conveyor appears to be jammed," Cabot said in that melodious voice so at odds with her severe appearance.

"Damn," Willa said, and headed toward the interior door. Cabot moved to open it for her. "Thanks."

Dorothy glared up at me. "What are you doing here?"

I held up the bag. "Getting tea."

"Hmmph. Cabot!"

Her nurse attendant returned and began pushing the chair. This time I hurried ahead to open it.

Once inside, I said, "Um, can you tell me where Iris lives? I want to stop by."

Dorothy waved at Cabot. "Tell her. Then come." And she pushed a button on her wheelchair. She jerked back as the chair took off toward the lobby.

I turned back to her nurse in amazement. "That thing's *motorized?*"

A wry smile quirked up one side of her mouth.

"Then why do you push it?"

"Because she tells me to."

"Because . . . but . . ." I trailed off.

Nurse Cabot's eyes glittered down at me. "Mrs. Swenson dislikes the motor. She also wants me to be nearby as much as possible, in case I'm needed. She pays me well to push that wheelchair around."

I could see deep lines around her eyes and mouth, and realized I'd never been this close to Dorothy's nurse. "Do you live with her?"

"For many years now. So you want to go to Quentin's house."

"Right. It's near here, isn't it? I thought I'd offer my condolences to his wife."

She gestured toward the hill that rose behind the meadery. "Take a right out of the parking lot and then the next right off the main road. Then a third right, and her house is on the left."

"Thanks."

"You're welcome." Task accomplished, she walked away without another word.

No questions, no personal comments, just pure professionalism. It seemed a lonely life, but what did I know? Perhaps Ms. Cabot had a riotous alter ego. And, as she pointed out, Dorothy paid her well.

■ ■ ■ ■

The road twisted and turned through the hemlock trees. I took right turn after right turn, but no house appeared. Cabot hadn't told me how far the house was from the main road. Tall trees grew right up to the shoulder of the narrow strip of pockmarked pavement. Overhead the sky had darkened again. I turned on the Rover's headlights.

Not that I needed to. There wasn't any other traffic.

My poor sense of direction had struck again; it was amazing how easily I could get lost. At a slightly wider stretch of shoulder, I pulled over as far as I could and dug out my cell phone. Only one bar out of five meant poor reception at best. All the stupid hills and trees didn't help. I didn't have Iris' number, so I dialed 411.

No Service popped up on the screen.

Great.

Okay. Her house might be farther down. I'd drive another quarter of a mile, and if I didn't find it I'd turn around, go home, and call Iris. I pulled back onto the road, accelerating a little faster than usual.

There. Up higher: a flash of sky reflected in a window. Finally.

The Land Rover ground up the steep driveway. At the top, more trees crowded up to a large manufactured home covered with dark green siding. No lawn. No yard, really, only the small circular driveway. Ivy crawled across the ground under the front windows and wound up the nearby tree trunks. It choked a rhododendron which stubbornly offered a few ragged red blooms anyway. The window blinds were closed. At the side of the house a boat trailer peeked out from beneath a blue tarp held down by dirty, five-gallon buckets filled with God knew what.

My encounters with Iris had been brief, but enough to get a clear impression of a put-together, creative woman with a distinct sense of style. She made contemporary quilts from hand-dyed silk, intended to hang on a wall, not cover a bed.

This was not the kind of place I'd ever have imagined her in. Quentin, either. The closed window blinds gave me pause, too. But Victoria's white VW Passat was parked on the gravel in front of the garage. Maybe the Leed's lawsuit had affected their finances to the degree that they couldn't keep up their house and yard. Or perhaps Iris' health wasn't as good as I'd been led to believe.

I parked in the circular drive and walked through the gloom to the door. Nothing seemed to happen when I pushed the button for the bell. I raised my hand to knock, then lowered it.

Something's wrong. Turn around. Go home. Call Iris on the phone.

I started to turn when I heard footsteps inside. The door opened.

Jakie looked almost as surprised to see me as I was to see him.

TWENTY-ONE

Suspicion and anger flared in his eyes before they narrowed to slits. His pockmarked face reddened. "You're the lady from the meadery. The one who can't find herself a restroom and ends up in the private offices instead."

Fear stabbed through me. "I, uh —"

Desperate, I tried to see into the interior gloom behind him. Where were Iris and Victoria?

He reached out a massive paw toward me. I ducked and stumbled backwards, heart hammering against my ribs. When I reached the gravel drive, my ankle twisted beneath me. The sudden shooting pain made me cry out. Arms pinwheeling, I almost went down.

Jakie lumbered across the threshold. I turned and half-ran, half-limped to my car, ankle screaming with every lurching step. Panic coursed through my veins. A primitive gibbering rose in my throat.

The afternoon had somehow taken a ter-rible, sickening turn. To what or where I didn't even know, but I didn't want to go there.

Move. Run. Faster.

I could feel him behind me, silent and enormous.

My hand was on the Land Rover's door handle when Jakie's thick fingers gripped my shoulder. I shrieked and pulled the door open. He spun me around, and my hand tore away from the car.

"What the hell are you doing here?"

My attempt to pull free was useless. "L . . . looking for Iris," I stammered, cran-ing my head back to look up at his face.

Jakie towered a good two feet over my five-six. Dark circles surrounded his blank, blue eyes under the shock of greasy black hair. His nostrils were so big I could practically see into his sinuses, and rank halitosis floated down to my level.

His slack face showed no reaction to my words.

I was shaking so badly I could barely stand. My throbbing ankle didn't help mat-ters. There was no way I could use either strength or speed to get away. Slowing my breath, I tried to get a grip on my voice.

"I came by to offer my condolences to

Iris." There: I didn't exactly sound casual, but at least the words sounded relatively even.

Still no response from Gigantor. My neck was starting to hurt, all bent back like that.

I tried again. "Iris Swenson? Quentin's wife? You know who Quentin was, right?"

He shook my shoulder. My teeth clattered together. "I'm not stupid, Miss Nosy Pants."

Miss Nosy Pants? Really?

I started to relax, but thought better of it when he grabbed the collar of my jacket and started pulling me toward the house.

Huh-uh. No way.

I dug my heels in, wincing at the fresh pain. "No, no, no. I know Victoria's here. That's her car. Call her out here. She knows me." Trying to sound reasonable, maybe make a bargain. Instead my voice was whiny and scared.

I didn't care. I *was* whiny and scared.

My tone didn't matter. Jakie was determined to take me inside. He yanked me along, yard by yard.

I twisted and thrashed the whole way.

"No. I. Won't. Go. In." Each word another step on the way to disaster.

I'm lost if he gets me on the other side of that door.

I raised my right foot, sagging against his

grip on my jacket to take the pressure off my bad left ankle, and kicked at his knee as hard as I could. He sidestepped me and held me at the end of his considerable reach. Gave me another teeth-rattling shake. I squirmed and fought, tried to slip out of my jacket, swung at his crotch with my fists. Effortlessly, he avoided my attempts to escape.

"Victoria!" I screamed. "Ir—"

He clamped his hand over my mouth. His enormous paw covered my whole face. Suddenly, I couldn't breathe.

We were at the door.

Jakie pushed me inside.

He slammed the door closed behind me.

Pinpricks of light floated across my vision, and my legs were growing weak as I fought for breath. Jakie didn't seem to notice, but his hand shifted the slightest amount.

Just enough: I bit him. Hard. His skin tasted metallic and bitter.

With an animal grunt, he pushed me away. My back hit the wall with a hollow thunk, knocking any remaining wind right out of me. The look he gave me before turning away held the promise of more pain.

I wheezed in a sip of air. Not enough. Steadying myself against the wall with my palms, I drew a long, shuddering inhalation. The overwhelming scent of cat pee almost brought me to my knees. My eyes started watering, tears streaming down my face.

Coughing and choking, now I didn't even want to breathe, but I still had to. God, how could anyone live in here?

"Don't yell," Jakie said. "Don't scream. Don't even talk. If you make a sound, I'll hit you."

A simple enough statement. I tipped my head forward in understanding, if not acceptance. A blow from Jakie would be like a wallop from the Incredible Hulk.

Reaching out that baseball mitt of a hand, he locked the door from the inside. New alarm bells started clanging, silent klaxons in my mind. Terror fractured my reason, made it hard to think.

He pointed at me. "Don't move."

Between the spasms of fear and the incredible stink, I realized I was very, very close to passing out.

No, no. Unacceptable. Bad thing to be unconscious now, here. Very bad.

Must breathe.

Yes. Good. Breathe again.

Ick.

My vision was blurry, but I could still see Jakie move to the other end of the room

222

and take a cell phone out of his pants pocket. It looked like a toy in his hand. How he was able to punch the tiny keys, I didn't know. He managed somehow and brought it to his ear.

Waited. Watching me.

I remained by the wall in the living room. My watering eyes began to adjust to the darkness. Outside, it was gray and cloudy. Inside, the covered windows created an artificial night, with a tiny sliver of illumination provided by a broken slat in the blinds. A torn recliner hunched in the middle of the room, facing a humongous flat screen television in the corner. I could see an empty dining room through an arched opening, and a hallway leading to what in a normal house would be bedrooms.

This was not a normal house. I had a pretty good suspicion, though, that it was Normal's house. Or one of them.

A sliding glass door on the far side of the dining room beckoned. It was hard to estimate how far I'd have to sprint on my bad ankle to get there, partly because I couldn't see very well to gauge distance. Then there was the heavy brocade curtain that blocked any view of the outdoors, so I didn't know what lay on the other side.

For a house without any furniture, this

one sure had the window coverings handled.

Through the dining room, I could also see part of another door that must have led to the kitchen. It was closed, but a thin band of yellow light shone from underneath the door.

What on earth had I stumbled into? I wouldn't have even stopped if Victoria's car hadn't been outside. But I had an awful feeling Victoria wouldn't be any help to me.

I coughed, the smell burning my throat now. There was no evidence of cats. Maybe this was a house Normal had repossessed, despite Felix's belief that he'd given up the real estate scam. Maybe the former owners had owned cats. Like eighty or ninety of them. And never let them outside. And didn't provide a litter box.

Right.

Ten feet away, the knob on the front door rattled.

I glanced up at Jakie. He frowned down at the floor. The phone was gone.

No Service . . .

He didn't hear the soft metallic sound as a key slid home. The snick of the lock disengaging. The muscles in my thighs bunched, ready. To hell with my ankle; this was my chance, and I'd run as hard as I could even if I broke it.

The door slammed open, and Normal stepped in. Our eyes locked, and his widened as his mouth opened in surprise.

"What the . . . ? Jakie!" he bellowed. "What is this woman doing in here?"

Jakie was across the room in two strides. "I tried to call. She just showed up out of the blue. I didn't know what she wanted. Didn't know what to do." Now Gigantor was the one who sounded whiny.

Normal, even shorter than me, glared up at him. "Did you bother asking her what she wanted, you big oaf? Go watch television."

They locked eyes for a long moment, something passing between them. Finally, they reached a silent agreement. Jakie shambled to the corner and folded himself into the recliner. The television clicked onto an infomercial for face cream and stayed there. He watched us.

I sidled toward the door, which Normal still blocked. He was wiry and looked strong in the way monkeys are strong. No doubt a chimpanzee, though smaller than me, could kick my butt. But a bald, eighty-something chimp? Given the circumstances, I was ready to take my chances.

"Good grief. You can't treat guests like that just because they come unannounced."

Normal turned to me and stuck out his hand.

I looked at it as if it held rat turds. How did he know how Jakie had treated me? Had he been watching? Did his lackey abduct visitors on a regular basis?

"Now c'mon, Miss. I'm sorry about my boy here." He dropped his voice. "He's a little paranoid."

Glancing up, I saw Jakie had heard. His eyes, so dead before, skittered to the left.

I suppressed a shudder. "I came to the wrong house. Got turned around and thought this was Quentin's place. Wanted to offer my condolences to his wife."

Normal's face lit up. "Well, that's awful nice of you. But you're right, little lady — this is the wrong address. Ha! Can you imagine Iris living in a dump like this?"

Silent, I shook my head. Eyed the doorway. My heart rate had slowed a bit, but I didn't trust either one of these yahoos any further than I could toss a Mack truck.

"What a mess!" he said. "See, the former renters were hard on the place. Me 'n' Jakie here are fixin' it back up for the next ones to come in. Sorry 'bout the confusion. Jakie don't mean no harm."

I made a noncommittal noise.

"So anyways, to get to Quentin's place,

you go down that road out front there to the left. And then take another left. It's a neat, blue-and-brick two-story with a nice big flower garden in front." His expression was condescending, implying I was an idiot for even stopping at this house.

But I was too scared to feel insulted. I fingered the Land Rover keys in my pocket, allowing a flicker of hope to surface that I'd actually be able to use them, and pasted a big smile on my face.

"Well, I did kind of wonder. But then I saw Victoria's car out front there, and Willa said she was with Iris, so I just kind of assumed . . ."

Something flickered in Normal's eyes. Out of the corner of my eye I saw Jakie's head turn toward me.

I forced perkiness into my voice. "But I've got a ton of work to get back to, so I'll give Iris a call from home. Such a shame what happened to Quentin."

"Yes, it surely is," Normal said, offering no explanation of where Victoria might be or why her car was parked in front of the garage.

And I wasn't about to ask. All I wanted was to get out of there.

He rubbed the rough stubble on his chin, the sandpapery noise audible above the prattling saleswoman on the television. "Quentin was way too young to go and die from a heart attack like that. And here I am, old as the hills and plugging right along. Must be all the clean livin'."

Jakie made an unpleasant noise.

Normal's knowing grin revealed yellowed dentures.

I smiled through gritted teeth. "Must be. I really do have to be going now, though."

He turned and held the door open for me. Quick as a bunny, I tried to slip by him, but his gnarled fingers gripped my elbow. "No harm, no foul, then. Right, little lady?"

Twisting my arm against his thumb, I broke his grip. We were eye to eye in the doorway for a long moment.

I looked away. "Right."

He didn't try to stop me as I limped past and out to the Land Rover, almost hyper-ventilating as I quietly sucked in the cool, clean air.

Fat raindrops spattered against the hood. Removing my keys from my pocket, I climbed in, shut the door and locked it. Normal stood in the open doorway, the wavering shadows cast by the television playing in the dark room behind him. I turned my head and met the old man's steady gaze.

The car started on the first try, thank God. Normal closed the door. Hot and more than a little bothered, I lowered the window to let in the humid breeze. The sound of yelling inside the house blended with the purr of the engine.

I made out the words "cop," "wife," and "idiot" before shifting into gear.

Twenty-Two

Left ankle throbbing, I managed to work the clutch well enough to get down the driveway without stalling out. I turned back toward the meadery, swearing under my breath at Cabot and her lousy directions. Guess it served me right, not calling Iris before heading over to her house.

The adrenaline began to fade, leaving me shaking from scalp to toe.

And my mind began to work.

Why had Jakie reacted so violently when I knocked on the door? He could have simply told me to go away. I would have happily skedaddled. But to drag me inside? What was that all about?

And that house! Normal's use of the word "mess" was the understatement of the year. The only way to make that place habitable would be to remove all trace of flooring and start over again. I bet even the paint on the walls smelled bad.

Sheesh.

The state patrol car came up behind the Land Rover fast and silent, red and blue lights flashing brightly against the afternoon gloom. I pulled to the side, sucking my breath in through my teeth in pain when I had to use the clutch to downshift.

The lights pulled in behind me.

What the . . . ?

Barr boiled out of the cruiser and ran to the Land Rover. The skin was drawn tight across his features, and worry radiated from his eyes. I lowered the window the rest of the way as he reached me.

"Are you okay?" were the first words out of his mouth.

I nodded. "How did you know?"

"You're really okay," he said, relaxing the tiniest amount.

"My ankle's twisted, but I'm all right. Honest."

He stared at me, then passed a hand over his face. When he looked back up at me the worry in his eyes had been joined by fury.

"God damn it, Sophie Mae!" he roared.

I flinched.

"What the *hell* were you thinking? Didn't I tell you specifically to stay away from Normal Brown?"

"But —"

231

"Didn't I ask you nicely to leave him out of your ridiculous little investigation?"

"But —"

"Didn't you *promise?*"

"I —"

"Why couldn't you once — just once — do as I asked? Have you any idea what you've done?"

I opened my mouth, intending to defend myself, but all that came out was a choked sob. And then another. All the fear and anger and desperation of the last hour came pouring out.

Barr yanked the door open and wrapped his arms around me.

"It was —" I managed, "an accident."

He patted me on the back. "I know."

"I didn't mean to," I gasped out.

More pats.

I squeezed my eyes shut and took a few deep, shuddering breaths. Willed away the sudden flood of tears. For the first time since Jakie opened that door, I felt truly safe.

"I didn't go there on purpose," I said.

"It's okay. Sorry I yelled. I was just so scared when they told me you were in there. Forgive me?"

Sniffling, I nodded my snotty nose wetly against his shoulder.

Wait a minute. What?

232

I pulled away and fumbled for a tissue. Blew my nose. Peered around my husband's shoulder at the patrol car behind us, the lights now blessedly off.

"Who told you I was at Normal's?"

"I'll explain later," Barr said.

My eyes, already swollen and red, narrowed. "Tell me now."

He sighed.

"Barr, what's going on?"

A pickup truck drove by, the occupants gawking at us, probably wondering what the tousled blond with the red nose had been up to that got her pulled over by the cops.

"Normal has been under surveillance for some time now. That's why I didn't want you to have anything to do with him. Not only is he dangerous, but we're developing a case against him that should put him away for a good long time. Probably the rest of his life."

"Murder?" I breathed.

His mouth twisted in a wry grimace. "No, dear. Not murder. That's your purview."

I ignored the sarcasm, looking back at the car behind us again. "Who —"

"Can you get home on your own?" he interrupted. "We need to get off this road."

"My ankle is pretty messed up. It's hard to shift, but I made it this far."

He shook his head. "I'll drive you. Hang on a minute." A few strides later he was talking to the driver behind us. I heard the other car's engine roar to life, and the sound of tires on gravel. As the patrol car passed by, the officer inside gave me a long, hard look.

Then Barr was back by my window. "Scoot over."

I scooted. He climbed in and adjusted the seat. We fastened our seat belts, and he pulled back onto the road.

"Where's your car?" I asked, meaning the department's unmarked Impala he usually drove.

"At the station. The lieutenant was there, and we came out here together when Robin called with the news that my wife was a possible hostage."

"Hostage? She really said that?"

His eyes cut toward me and then back to the road. "Jakie's frighteningly volatile — anything could have been going on."

I swallowed, forcing my dry throat to work. I'd been really scared, but maybe not scared enough. A sudden weariness descended over me, and my eyes closed for a long moment. The pain in my ankle flared every time my heart beat, a throbbing reminder of my close brush with violence.

Opening my eyes, I slid my seat back and put my foot up on the dash. My ankle had swollen to twice its normal size and turned a lovely shade of purple.

"Who's the lieutenant? And why are you guys working outside of the city limits?"

"It's a multi-jurisdictional case, so we're working with both the sheriff's department and Washington state patrol." He glanced over at me, probably weighing what to say.

I waited, too exhausted to quiz him.

"Since there are only two detectives on the Cadyville force, we're working on this thing pretty much full time and fitting in our other cases around it."

"No wonder you've been so tired lately."

"It'll be worth it in the long run. We're gathering more evidence every day. Do you remember the Morton case? The one the judge threw out because the confession wasn't clear on the recording and Morton wouldn't sign the transcript?"

"Of course I remember. The guy who was selling drugs at the high school. That's the whole reason you wanted those mini-cassettes in the first place."

"Believe me, I'm aware of the irony. No way would you have been inside Normal Brown's house if it hadn't been for those stupid tapes."

I waved my hand in front of my face, remembering. "God, it was awful in there. So Normal's involved with drugs at the high school like Morton was?"

"He's involved with Morton — and some other people. I'll tell you more when I can, but we're trying to keep all this on a need-to-know basis. Maybe I should've told you this much before, but I was trying to keep you as far away from the situation as possible."

"But I didn't know I would be breaking my promise to stay away from Normal."

"And Jakie."

"And Jakie," I agreed. "I was looking for Quentin's house, to drop by and see whether I could do anything for his widow. I'd never have gone to the door of that miserable dump if Willa hadn't told me her sister was at Iris' house. Victoria's Passat was right there in the driveway, so I figured it had to be the right place."

His face cleared. "That makes perfect sense."

"Well, I'm glad something does."

"If it makes you feel any better, Victoria was indeed at Iris' house. Which is quite close to Normal's house. The one he actually lives in. His truck had a flat tire, so he borrowed her car to come over to the drug house."

"Boy, that's some surveillance you have on him."

"Him and Jakie, both. Mostly on the house you just escaped from."

Escaped from. God. "Which you just called 'the drug house.' "

We'd reached the edge of Cadyville. Barr slowed to a sedate twenty-five miles an hour.

"I guess I did." He was quiet for a moment. "What did you see in there?"

"Nothing," I said.

"Nothing at all?"

"It's empty except for a chair and a TV. No other furniture that I saw. Nothing on the walls. No lamps. It was dark. The blinds and curtains were all closed."

He nodded. "They would be."

"But there's nothing to see in there. Of course, I was only in the living room. Never saw into the bedrooms or the kitchen."

Relief flooded his face. "You didn't see into the kitchen at all?"

I shook my head. "Nuh uh. The door was closed. All I could see was the light on under the door."

"Good."

"Good? I'd rather be able to help you."

"I'm glad you can't. That way Normal

won't have any reason to keep you quiet."

A shiver ran through me. I rolled up my window. Sniffed my jacket. "I don't know how they can stand to be in there with all the windows shut like that. The stink was so bad it made my eyes water. I can still smell it on my jacket. Cat pee."

He pulled my other arm over to his face as we pulled up in front of the Drop-In Clinic. "Let me smell."

"Weirdo."

He let go of my arm and straightened. "Ammonia." He met my eyes. "The telltale smell of a meth lab."

TWENTY-THREE

"It's just a sprained ankle," I told the curly haired doctor. "There's nothing to do about it except ice it and wait."

"Stop telling her how to do her job," Barr said from his position by the door of the examining room.

In the car, I'd argued against medical attention and lost. At least my concerned hubby hadn't insisted on taking me to the hospital in a neighboring town. The Drop-In Clinic was as good as it got in Cadyville, which was fine with me.

Doctor Freeman bent over my foot, propped on a stool in front of me, probing and rotating and saying, "Hmm. Mmm, hmm," under her breath. She looked up. "Yeah, it's sprained all right."

"See? I told you. Ice and wait." And slather copious amounts of arnica salve on it.

A smile tugged at her lips. "Ice, elevate,

and wait. You're going to have to stay off this. I'm giving you crutches."

"Oh, for heaven's sake."

"Sophie Mae . . ." Barr's tone held warning.

"Fine." I forced a smile. My energy was returning as the adrenalin backlash evened out in my bloodstream. "Crutches it is." I glanced at my watch. "Penny was due at the house fifteen minutes ago. I'm sure she's waiting."

The clinic set me up with a pair of crutches, and I swung my way back out to the Land Rover. On the way home, Barr called the station and arranged for a patrol car to pick him up and take him back to work. It was waiting behind my employee's PT Cruiser in front of the house when we got there.

Penny flung her car door open before we had even stopped. Radiating agitation, she marched up to the window. "Sophie Mae, if I'm going to be kept waiting like this, I —" Coming face-to-face with Barr brought her up short. "Oh . . ."

"You must be Penny," he said. "I'm Sophie Mae's husband." He stuck his hand through the opening.

She took it without a word.

"I'm afraid it's my fault that Sophie Mae's

late. I insisted we have her ankle looked at before coming home."

On the other side of the Rover, I wrestled crutches, tote, and self to the sidewalk.

Penny craned her neck, trying to see me better. "Her ankle? What happened?"

"Just a little sprain," I called. "Be with you in a jif."

Awkwardly working the crutches, I managed something that faintly resembled a rhythm. At least I hadn't fallen down using the darn things.

Yet.

"Don't worry," I said to Penny. "I'll pay you for your time. And there's plenty to do inside, so if you want to stay an hour later, that's fine, too."

"Oh, no, no, I couldn't possibly do that. In fact, I'll have to leave early today."

The crutches stilled. "What?"

"Robbie — my youngest?" Gone was the agitation, replaced by delight.

I nodded. The one who couldn't walk two blocks to a gas station.

Barr had gotten out and was waiting. I held up a finger. "Hang on just a second, Penny." Turning to him, I said, "I'll be fine."

"You sure?"

"Positive. Go ahead. Catch the bad guys."

He came up and wrapped his arms around

me, right in front of Officer Dawson still waiting in the car and Penny gawping at us from the sidewalk.

"I'll see you tonight," he whispered in my ear. "Don't get into any trouble before then, okay?"

I laughed — sort of. Hadn't he said that yesterday? "I'll do my best."

"Hmmph." He strode to the police car and got in. They drove away. I watched them go most of the way down the block before turning back to my employee. Who had been telling me she had something better to do than actually work for me that afternoon.

"You two are so cute!" she gushed. "My husband would no more kiss me on the street than he'd drop his pants."

Good to know.

"So. Robbie," I prompted.

"Yes. He's looking for a job, you see. Now, we've told him his job is to go to the community college and get good grades. To concentrate on his schoolwork, and we'd pay for his apartment and living expenses." She paused.

I began to shuffle up the walk, desperately hoping she would get to the point.

She fell in beside me. "He wants to get a job anyway. Says he's too old to have us paying for everything."

"How old is he?" I asked, mentally kicking myself for extending the story.

"Twenty-seven."

Oh, good Lord.

"That seems old enough to make your own money," I ventured.

She sighed. "I suppose you're right. At any rate, he's filling out job applications this afternoon."

I waited. She beamed at me. Finally I said, "And . . . ?"

"And I need to leave early to help him."

That seemed like a good time to try putting some weight on my left foot. The pain shooting through my ankle successfully distracted me from saying what I was thinking.

"When were you thinking of going?" I asked instead.

She looked at her watch and then up at me with regret. "I thought I'd stay an hour, but now it will have to just be half an hour or so."

That would be about enough time for her to package a dozen lotion bars.

"Tell you what. Why don't you take the rest of the afternoon off? No sense getting started on something and then having to leave in the middle."

A sunny smile at that. "Well, I think you're right about that, dear. And that way you can take the afternoon off, too. Take care of that ankle of yours."

"Mmm." No way could I afford to take the afternoon off — especially now.

Sheesh.

"What happened to your ankle, anyway?"

"I sprained it," I said, unwilling to give her any gossip fodder. Not that it would matter in the long run. I wondered what story she'd come up with to spread around.

For once, whatever it was, I doubted it would be nearly as salacious as the actual truth.

I tossed the crutches on the bench in the foyer and hopped on one foot into the bathroom to retrieve the arnica salve. Back on the sofa, I carefully rubbed it on my swollen ankle, drawing the lavender scent into my lungs. The enormity of what really could have happened to me hit once I was alone. Thank God, Penny had gone. I simply couldn't deal with her on top of everything else right now.

Ice. I needed ice. And to elevate my foot.

Now how the heck was I going to do that and get anything done? Anxiety flittered against my rib cage. I had to get those orders out. All by myself, since Cyan had a little do tonight called prom and Penny, bless her absence, was, well . . . absent.

A nice big handful of painkillers might come in handy. I wondered whether Victoria had any OxyContin to spare.

When the doorbell rang, I might have ignored it if Brodie hadn't gone nuts with the barking.

"Shhh," I said, and got to my feet.

Or foot, rather.

Gingerly, I put a tiny bit of weight on my bad ankle and found I could bear it if I limped heavily. Uncomfortable but doable. Good. No way could I wrestle a pair of crutches up and down the stairs to my workroom.

Ruth Black stood on the front step. "Sophie Mae, honey, what's wrong?" She bustled in. "Thaddeus gave me your message yesterday, and I didn't hear back from you so I thought I'd just drop by since I was out running errands. You look terrible!"

"Thanks, Ruth," I said with a rueful grin. I limped back into the living room.

She grabbed my elbow after a few steps. Her spiked white hair had been freshly trimmed to an inch long, her eyes twinkled concern at me, and her long, batik-print skirt swished between us as she guided me to the sofa. She was surprisingly strong for a seventy-one-year-old.

"What happened?"

"I sprained my ankle."

She gave me a look. "No kidding?"

I eased onto a chair. "Let's just say I chose the wrong gravel driveway to run on."

Her eyes flicked to her watch. "I know there's more to it. Have you been up to one of your investigations again? That's when you usually get hurt."

At my studied lack of response, she smiled brightly and went on. "Is that why you want to know about Elizabeth Moser?"

I leaned forward. "So you did know her."

"Just a bit. We chatted a few times at the spinning guild meetings. I'm surprised you never met her."

That triggered my guilt reflex. "I've been so busy I haven't gone to a meeting for over three months."

"Well, that explains it then. She only joined the guild two months ago."

"I saw Elizabeth had a stash, but didn't see a wheel. So she was a spinner."

"Liked the drop spindle best. Good knitter, too," Ruth said. "It's such a shame what happened. She was far too young to die."

"Do you know if she had a heart condition?" I asked.

She shook her head. "It was so strange. A heart attack, of all things, coming out of the blue like that. I mean, Elizabeth was a jogger. I personally don't understand the idea of running around for no good reason, but she said it was as good for her mind as it was for her body. She kept quite fit."

That didn't guarantee she hadn't died from natural causes. Athletes had been struck down before. Still, I didn't buy it, not after Quentin Swenson's oddly timed heart attack.

I sat back. "Okay, spill all you know about her."

"Tell me what this is about first."

I considered. "I came across some used tapes from her practice at the thrift store. I listened to them, and when I realized what they were I was going to give them back to her. But she'd already died. Her voice, the things she said . . . and now I find out she was a spinner. I wish I'd had a chance to meet her." I looked down. "Sounds pretty weird, huh."

Ruth's gaze held sympathy. "I think I understand." She slipped off her sandals and tucked her feet up under her on the sofa. "Let's see. I've only spoken with her a few times." She began ticking off her fingers. "Forty-two, nasty divorce from a man who

247

cheated on her, no children, a sister in Tacoma, parents live in Florida, doesn't get along with her father, likes jogging, Indian food, educated as an interior designer, got a job as a web designer and changed careers when she moved to Cadyville." She ran out of fingers and dropped her hands. "She was a sweet girl, and loved the idea of helping people. I liked her a lot. Most of the spinning guild showed up for her funeral, and I met her sister." Ruth wrinkled her nose. It was enough to convey how the sister had impressed her. Or rather had not impressed her.

That reminded me. "Her neighbor said Elizabeth's sister was going to put her collection of craft supplies — which I assume meant her yarn and fiber — on Craigslist. I got her phone number." I stood and gimped over to my tote bag. Found the number and copied it down for Ruth. "I thought you or one of your knitting friends might be interested."

She took the slip of paper. "You're not?"

"I still have so many of those beautiful yarns and rovings you helped Barr pick out last year." He'd surprised me with the Land Rover full of gorgeous fiber and my very own spinning wheel right before asking me to marry him.

"Hi, Ruth!" Erin walked in the door, backpack swinging from one hand. "Guess what?"

"What?" Ruth responded dutifully.

"We're making dandelion wine tonight. Ginger ale, too."

"That's terrific," Ruth said. "Uncle Thaddeus used to make elderberry wine every year, but he stopped awhile back. Maybe I'll light a fire under him to do it again this summer."

"Oh, no," I groaned. "I totally forgot. Sorry, Bug, but I'm going to have to call Tootie and cancel."

The look on her face would have beat Brodie's best sad eyes any day.

I pointed to my foot. "I sprained my ankle today."

"But I can do all the work. All you'll have to do is sit there. Pleasepleaseplease?"

"Why are you so excited?" I asked. "You told me once you thought all this old-fashioned pioneer stuff I do is weird."

She shrugged. "It is. But it's kind of cool, too. And I really want to see Nana Tootie. It's been ages."

It had been quite awhile since she'd spent any time with her great-grandmother. I saw Tootie more often because I dropped by Caladia Acres when Erin was in school.

249

"We'll have to stick with the ginger ale, then, since I can't really go pick dandelions with you."

"Nonsense," Ruth said. "I know the perfect place. It's a field chock full of dandelions in bloom, away from the road and I know the farmer doesn't use chemicals on his pasture. Erin, put on some shoes you don't mind getting dirty, and we'll go right now."

Erin hurried down the hallway to her room.

"Oh, Ruth. You don't have to —" I began to protest.

She cut me off. "It won't take long. Just have me over for a glass of wine when it's ready."

"You got it. And thank you."

When they had gone, I weighed my options. I still needed to finish packaging the lotion bars, pack up two wholesale orders and label another gross of lye soap. Dinner needed to be quick and simple. I limped into the kitchen and rummaged through the pantry. We still had a half a dozen jars of home-canned tomato sauce from last summer's garden. Spaghetti it would be, with a big salad from the garden. Erin could harvest the greens when she got back from picking dandelions.

In the meantime, a handful of aspirin would have to get me through the rest of the afternoon.

TWENTY-FOUR

"I do believe that tea works," Tootie said from across the butcher block table.

Her cane leaned against the edge, next to her chair. Felix sat beside her, across from Barr, and Erin sat at the end. We were all digging into the pile of pasta, sauce, and baked meatballs.

"Then you'll be pleased to know that I got more from Victoria today. Or Willa, rather. Victoria wasn't at the meadery."

Barr looked at me and gave a little shake of his head. Did he think I was going to talk about the meth lab? Please. But then he said, "I don't think you should drink any of that tea, Tootie. In fact, I'd like to take it with me, have it tested."

Erin stopped chewing and stared at him. She wasn't the only one.

"What are you talking about?" I asked.

"We got preliminary toxicology results back this afternoon."

"On Quentin?"

"No. On the bottle of mead that was sitting on the coffee table next to him when he died."

I put my fork down. "And?"

"And they found a compound that induces slow paralysis and then stops the heart. There was a sufficient amount that one glass of mead would have killed him."

Felix, unaccustomed to the kind of dinnertime conversation popular at our house, gaped at him.

"Did kill him, you mean," I said.

Barr nodded. "Looks like it. The lab found, let me see here." He fumbled a notebook out of his pocket. "Conium alkaloids in the bottle."

"What the heck is that?" Felix asked.

"They originate in *conium maculatum*," he read, then looked up. "That's apparently the Latin name for poison hemlock."

"*What?* You mean the stuff they killed Socrates with?" I asked.

"You said Victoria has a big herb garden at the meadery," he continued. "You were looking up some of the poisonous plants there the other night."

"Yes."

"Did you see anything that looked like poison hemlock?"

253

"Barr, I have no idea what poison hemlock looks like. I mean, that's pretty obscure."

"Actually you can find it in ditches and fields all around here," Tootie said, exuding serenity despite all the talk of poisons and death.

"Well, at any rate, it's not something you just pick up at the drugstore," Barr said. "We'll be taking a look at that garden. In the meantime, I'd like to take that tea to the lab and have it tested as well."

Felix looked worried.

"You don't think it's poisonous, do you?" Tootie asked. "Because it's done wonders for my joint pain."

"I think it's a good idea to test it," I said. I didn't think it was poisonous, but it did occur to me that Victoria might have added some of her magic OxyContin to the mixture to ensure some additional relief.

"I agree, Petunia," Felix said. "Better to be safe than sorry."

Tootie sighed. "If you think that's best."

"I can't quite wrap my mind around why either Victoria or Willa would kill their brother," I said.

Barr held a palm up to the ceiling. "We just don't have enough information yet. But we will, don't worry." He turned his hand over and pointed at me. "And by 'we' I

254

mean the police, not the Ambroses."

"Petunia told me you were asking questions about the Swenson family because that shrink died," Felix whispered. "I heard some gossip the other day you might be interested in."

My gaze shot across the room to Erin, who was carefully measuring out sugar and powdered ginger under her grandmother's tutelage. Barr had gone upstairs to check his e-mail at work, and Felix and I sat at the table, busily stripping the bright yellow petals from the pile of freshly washed dandelion flowers. Tootie had said we'd need eight cups. We were about halfway there.

"Is it something Erin shouldn't hear?" I whispered back.

Both Tootie and Erin turned and looked at me. I guess my whisper needed a little work.

"Naw. It's just, you know . . ."

I raised my eyebrows.

". . . gossip."

My lips twitched as I realized he was more interested in keeping his predilection for rumor mongering quiet around Tootie. "Right. Well, I think we can make the argument that in this case it's for a good cause."

He brightened at that. "Well, the other day I was sitting in the recreation room, and Dorothy Swenson was there with a couple of her friends."

"Felix likes to hang out with the ladies, you know," Tootie teased.

"Oh, Petunia, you know it's not like that. Anyway they were talking about their grandchildren. Betsy Maher — you know her, don't you?"

I nodded. Her son was Cadyville's police chief, and Betsy loved to get the lowdown on local goings-on from her son.

"Well, she said that her daughter lives in Phoenix, and her son — Betsy's grandson — moved back in with his parents at the tender age of thirty-eight."

Echoes of my earlier conversation with Penny Turner came to mind.

Felix bent toward me. "Dorothy jumps in then and says how she's got four grandchildren — that was before Quentin died, of course — that she has to take care of."

"Take care of? Did she refer to anything specifically?"

He nodded vigorously. "She said she'd been keeping that wine shop downtown afloat ever since it opened. That she'd told Glen she wasn't going to keep him in business anymore. She gave him one more year to make a real go of the place, and if he didn't then he'd have to close it up."

"I wondered how a fancy wine store could make any money in a little town like Cadyville." I shifted my foot, propped on a pillow on the chair opposite. "Apparently it doesn't. I suppose that might give Glenwood a motive to kill Dorothy. But she's not the one who died."

Felix looked a little disappointed.

"Now mix the sugar and ginger into the water until the sugar dissolves," Tootie told Erin. "When it does, just let it sit on the counter with a thin layer of cheesecloth over it. Every day for a week, add another teaspoon of sugar and another of ginger. It should start to bubble. Then I'll tell you what to do next."

She came and sat down with us, reaching for a dandelion. "You know, all those grandkids of hers get the same amount of Dorothy's money when she dies. She's made no secret that her will divides the pie up equally."

My fingers slowed. "Now that might be a reason for one of his siblings to kill Quentin. After all, if one of them is dead, the others get more money when Grandma kicks off."

Felix waggled his eyebrows, but Tootie

looked concerned. "That's terrible."

"It also means the killer may not be done," Barr said from the doorway, where he'd obviously been listening.

I motioned him back into the kitchen. "Now that you have the results back on Quentin's bottle of mead, can you get access to the mead I saw through Elizabeth Moser's window?"

He looked thoughtful. "I can try."

"Tonight?"

"First thing in the morning." He saw the disappointment on my face. "I promise."

"If she was cremated, then testing those bottles may be the only way to prove Elizabeth was murdered." I patted the chair beside me.

Barr sat down.

"We were just talking about Dorothy's will. How much of a motive is the money, anyway?" I asked. "I mean, is she really that rich?"

"She's worth about four million," Barr said. "Not including Grendel. The meadery will be divided equally among the grandchildren, but she told me her will stipulates none of them can sell their portion unless it's to the other siblings."

"What about Quentin's share?"

"His share of the meadery goes to Iris.

But the liquid assets will now be redistributed among Victoria, Willa, and Glenwood."

Tootie stood again. "All right. Enough of this talk. Let's get some water boiling so we can steep these petals."

"Why?" Erin asked.

"Because dandelion wine starts with dandelion tea."

Erin carefully wrote that down.

"Then we'll add sugar and let that dissolve, and when it's cooled down a bit, the yeast will go in."

"Uh-oh," I said. "Will bread yeast work?"

"In a pinch, but the result won't be as nice," Tootie said. "Your husband here stopped at Berries and Hops on the way over from Caladia Acres, though, so we could pick up a white wine yeast."

I smiled at Barr. "Thanks."

The next hour felt like plain, ordinary family time.

For once.

As soon as Barr had left to take Tootie and Felix back to Caladia Acres, I asked Erin to fill the dishwasher. Then I settled in on the sofa with my foot up and all the herbal references in the house piled around me.

It didn't take long to find a picture of poison hemlock. And it looked disturbingly familiar. In fact, it looked exactly like the plant which that very morning I'd been trying to decide was either thick-stemmed parsley or thin-stalked celery.

Good Lord. I'd been ready to pick some of it. No wonder Willa had sounded sharp.

Wait a second. The pictures.

I hobbled into the foyer and extracted the cell phone from my big tote bag on the bench. Back on the sofa, I flipped through the shots I'd taken.

There: poison hemlock.

Victoria had mentioned that wine was the best thing to extract the medicinal properties of herbs. Honey wine would certainly qualify. And it would be easy for her to repackage a tainted bottle. All those swing-top Grendel bottles had nothing but a shrink-wrapped top to ensure the seal hadn't been broken. I had a pile of the same shrink-wrap bands down in my workroom; it was nothing to take one off and replace it with another. All you needed was the band and a hair dryer.

Erin came in and plopped on the sofa beside me. "Spaghetti sure can be messy."

"Mm, hmm." I was still distracted.

" 'Course, it's only my favoritest meal ever, so I don't mind."

I looked down at her. "Favoritest?"

She grinned.

"How'd your history project go? Didn't you have to do a presentation today?"

"Yeah. No biggie. Can I watch TV?"

"For an hour." Meghan was strict about limiting television time, but Erin was usually too busy with other things to push the limits.

"Okay." She reached for the remote control and turned on some ghastly reality show.

I left her to it and went downstairs to package soap. I heard Barr come back, and after a bit went up to make sure Erin had shut off the television. She was already in bed, but instead of her usual pre-sleep reading, she was writing furiously in her notebook.

" 'Night," I said.

She didn't look up. " 'Night."

Oh, well. It was Friday night. She could work on her book all night if she wanted to.

Upstairs, I showed Barr the pictures of the poison hemlock in the book and then the ones I'd taken with my cell phone.

"Nice work," he said, his chin on my shoulder. "Can you e-mail those to me?"

"Be glad to. Do you really think it was Victoria?"

"Or Willa."

"Glenwood's no slouch when it comes to knowledge about mead, and he's at Grendel a lot. He'd have access to the herb garden, too." But even as I said the words they felt like a stretch.

Barr murmured agreement, eyelids already drooping. I was exhausted, too, and my ankle throbbed. So much for the fabulous newlywed sex life. It had been nearly a week.

"You know," I said. "It occurs to me that Victoria might have another motive for killing Quentin."

"Mmm?"

"Maybe he wanted to stop providing her OxyContin. After all, with the lawsuit and the bill before the state legislature, he was probably under a lot of scrutiny. Warren Kringle would be keeping a keen eye on him, too. I'm surprised he managed to keep his job at the drugstore through all that."

"Do you know that he gave it to her illegally?"

"Well, no. But she made such a big deal about curing herself with herbs. Of course, talking the talk and walking the walk are two different things." I frowned. "Maybe she does have a valid prescription."

"It's a thought," Barr said. "Now stop thinking and come to bed."

It turned out he wasn't as tired as I

thought. And neither was I.

But three a.m. found me back down in my workroom packing the final box of Winding Road products to ship out the next day. Well, technically the same day.

Heavy footsteps on the stairs surprised me, and I whirled to find Barr standing at the bottom of the steps.

"What are you doing?" he asked.

"Why aren't you asleep?" I asked.

"I was until my phone rang. Have you been down here all night?"

"Not all night." I winked.

"Honey, you have to get some sleep."

"I was just coming up."

"And I have to go out now," he said.

I limped over, and he helped me get up the stairs. "Where are your crutches?"

"Can't maneuver with them. I'm fine. I take it the phone call is the reason you're going out?"

"Someone found a car on fire northeast of town."

I stopped halfway up the stairs, my hand on his arm. "Northeast?"

He nodded. "Near the Grendel meadery."

I had a bad feeling. "Not your jurisdiction, is it?"

"The troopers ran the plates on the car.

263

It's registered to Victoria Swenson."

Great. Like I was going to be able to sleep now.

TWENTY-FIVE

Exhaustion helped. Unconsciousness swept over me moments after I lay down. Unfortunately, it only lasted about an hour before worry tore me back to awareness. The sky outside my window began to lighten. I fluffed my pillow and flopped onto my back, staring at the ceiling. My ankle throbbed quietly beneath the covers, the pain almost like an old friend now. Thoughts stormed though my mind, unbidden and unorganized. I struggled to wrestle them into some kind of order.

Elizabeth Moser, starting a new life after a bad divorce, in a new town with a new profession. Alone, but connected to other fiber artists. Uneducated as a therapist but relying on practical common sense to help her vulnerable clients. Afraid but resolute, ready to tell the police and the Swenson family they might be in danger. Dead from a heart attack in her home, discovered by a pizza delivery boy.

Quentin Swenson, dead from a heart attack in his living room after drinking a glass of mead. Before his demise, he'd been a friendly pharmacist indirectly involved in a young woman's death, a dark cloud of a lawsuit shadowing his reputation. Reluctant connections to the family business, but his wife, recently in remission, worked there, and they lived practically next door to the meadery.

Not that I'd been able to find their house.

Dorothy Swenson, imperious and demanding, orchestrating the whole family. Keeping them close with promises of money, dictating decisions, barking orders at Normal, at Glenwood, at her assistant, Cabot.

Cabot. No one ever called her anything else. I wondered what her first name was. She looked like a Margaret, an Inga, or a Helga. How had she come to be in Dorothy's employ? She must have a special relationship with the Swenson matriarch to be able to spend so much time with her. Live with her. Over fifteen years, Glenwood had said the other day in A Fine Body. Dorothy seemed to respect her, though — certainly more than she did Glenwood himself. Maybe it was easier not to be one of Dorothy's family members.

But maybe Glenwood would have engendered more of his grandmother's respect if he'd managed to run his business without her help or her money. If he wasn't such a sycophantic little weasel when he was around her. I found it disappointing that his temperament and personality were at such unfortunate odds with his devastating good looks; Dorothy's disappointment must run much deeper.

Then there was Victoria, in her late forties the oldest of the four grandchildren, a divorced and remarried empty nester still mothering her siblings. Also a master herbalist, sanctimonious about using natural means to control her arthritis while downing the OxyContin. OxyContin provided by her brother Quentin — either illegally or with a valid prescription. Either way, he knew her secret.

How did that painkiller affect her? She'd never struck me as someone who was high. Just sad, sometimes. And certainly in pain. But could the pills be the reason she'd run her car into the ditch tonight?

More like this morning. Gray hints of future blue sky winked at me through the window. The clock on the bedside stand said 5:34.

Her sister Willa, on the other hand, seemed happy. She had a girlfriend and enjoyed being up to her earlobes in meadery business. She appeared to be the only normal, well-adjusted one. I instinctively trusted her, a feeling I instinctively distrusted. None of these people were turning out to be what I'd thought they were at first.

And speaking of normal, how about Dorothy's brother? What a character. No, that made him sound irascible yet adorable — like Felix. Normal, old-timey moonshiner turned mortgage scammer and drug kingpin. Cadyville might be a small kingdom indeed, but people here were just as damaged as anywhere else when it came to drugs like meth.

If Normal was the kingpin, Jakie was his jester. His relationship to the others was still unclear to me. Glenwood had referred to him as Normal's lackey, and he'd certainly seemed to fill that role the previous afternoon. Yes, he was definitely on the outside of things, yet up to his tweaked-out eyeballs in the drug business.

I shivered, remembering how he'd grabbed me and how helpless I'd felt. What would have happened if Normal hadn't come in and told him to let me go? I still wasn't sure why he had.

Then I remembered him yelling at Jakie as I left. He'd known who I was. And who Barr was.

Did he also know he was being watched? Did he know my husband was part of the team trying to put him behind bars? I wouldn't have been surprised. Normal was mean and lucky, but also smart and wily.

And let's not forget the poison hemlock found in Quentin's mead — and photographed by yours truly in the meadery herb garden. Willa had a deep interest in herb-laced honey wine. Victoria's extensive knowledge of herbs surely covered poison hemlock. Both had opportunity since they worked in the herb garden. Of the two, I'd go with Victoria as the killer, and I had the feeling Barr was more interested in her, too.

But all of the Swensons had access to the garden. Even Iris.

Head pounding from too much information and not enough sleep, I sat up and put my feet on the floor.

And thought about the bottles of mead I'd seen in the closet with Elizabeth's fiber stash. Would a toxicology report on those show hemlock as well? I was willing to bet the farm that it would. But what if Barr couldn't get a warrant for them? What if they weren't there anymore? What if the

269

sister had given everything away already?

Or worse, what if she took a nip out of Elizabeth's bottle?

I stood, slipped on my ducky slippers and shuffled to the bedroom door. I knew where Elizabeth's mead was. If I came in through the alley, especially this early in the morning, Elizabeth's neighbors probably wouldn't see me. And if they did, well, Barr could —

My thoughts screeched to a halt. Not only would Barr kill me if I got caught breaking and entering, but it was possible that acquiring the mead that way would eliminate it as viable evidence, even if it had enough poison hemlock in it to kill all the residents in Cadyville.

In the bathroom, I downed more aspirin, praying it would kick in quickly. My ankle had stopped throbbing, but it still hurt like the dickens to walk on. I lurched downstairs to the living room. My plant books were still scattered everywhere. I found the one that had the most information in it about poison hemlock and searched for the physical effects.

Dizziness, nausea, vomiting, then slow paralysis moving inward from the extremities until the lungs and heart stopped working.

Poor Quentin. Poor Elizabeth. Heck, poor Socrates.

Erin was still asleep when the front door opened and closed. Brodie lay in the hallway where he could keep an eye on the doors to the kitchen and her bedroom and now sprang to his stubby legs in order to greet Barr.

I was two cups of coffee into my morning and considering a third. Mushrooms, peppers, and onions, already browned, waited in the skillet on the stove. Rye bread poked up from the slots in the toaster, butter at the ready. Bacon was piled high on a plate on the table, the smoky aroma combining with the scent of rosemary and new potatoes roasting in a hot oven.

After being out most of the night, I figured Barr would be hungry. When he walked into the kitchen, I met him with a steaming cup of black coffee and a kiss.

"Thanks." He slumped into a chair and took a sip.

His eyes were red, and the gray stubble on his cheeks betrayed his age. I wanted to wrap my arms around him and make it better, but we were grownups and that didn't work anymore.

Instead, I poured my third cup and sat

down across from him. "Is she dead?"

He looked up. "Who?"

"Victoria."

He shook his head. "No. She wasn't in the car." Something in his voice.

I waited.

"Jakie was. And yes, he's dead."

"Jakie," I breathed. "That's . . . well, I don't really know what that is."

Barr blinked bleary eyes at me. Poor guy.

"Hungry?" I asked.

"I could eat a whole cow."

"Hmm. All I can offer is pig."

"I'll take it." And he did, snagging a piece of bacon from the plate on the table and biting into it.

I got up, limped to the stove and warmed the vegetables in the pan. I whipped the eggs with a fork and poured them in, punched down the lever on the toaster, and removed the potatoes, brown and puffy, from the oven. The fact that I was walking on my bad ankle didn't elicit a single comment from my hubbie, testimony to his physical and mental exhaustion.

A couple minutes stirring the eggs, a quick butter of the rye toast, and I set a steaming plate in front of my husband.

Sitting down again, I asked, "Why was Jakie in Victoria's car?"

"Mmmph," Barr said around a mouthful of potatoes and eggs.

"Was it an accident?"

He shook his head. Took another bite.

"Did she kill him?" After all, she was currently the prime suspect in her brother's death. But how she'd manage to kill that behemoth I couldn't imagine.

Oh, wait. Poison, of course.

But Barr wagged his chin in the negative again.

I tried again. "Was it supposed to be her in the car?"

He swallowed and rubbed his eyes with his fingers. "I don't think Victoria Swenson had anything to do with it. See, the surveillance team never saw Normal return her car. He had it ever since you saw it in the driveway of the meth house yesterday afternoon."

"So . . . Jakie was driving it in the middle of the night and ran into the ditch?" I was still trying for the accident angle, afraid of the alternative.

"Not exactly." His expression was grim. "Not unless he was driving with a fatal gunshot wound in his chest."

TWENTY-SIX

"Someone shot Jakie." The concept was disturbing, of course, but I didn't exactly feel deep mental anguish at the thought of his exit from this world.

"Not someone. Normal Brown." He forked in another bite, smaller this time.

"Did the surveillance team see him do it?" I asked.

A big swallow of orange juice then, "No." A lot of gloom in that single syllable. "They weren't paying enough attention at two thirty in the morning. Granted, there's never been much activity then, but still. Normal and Jakie both slipped out. Must have walked to the meth lab — they sleep at Normal's house, which I mentioned is near Quentin's."

I nodded that I remembered. I wondered how Iris, all alone now, liked having Great Uncle Normal living next door.

"Somehow he got Jakie in the car. He shot

him either before or after running the car into the ditch. Then he set the whole thing on fire, probably hoping evidence of the murder would be erased by the heat. Heck, it might have worked if another driver hadn't seen the fire right away, driven up there, and hit it with an extinguisher before the fire department arrived."

"Why are you so sure it was Normal who killed him? I mean, they were dealing drugs, right? Isn't sudden death kind of an occupational hazard in that line of work?"

He snorted an unamused laugh. "I won't rule it out. But I think Normal killed Jakie because he'd been sampling the product. Addiction to methamphetamine occurs very quickly. Jakie was becoming a liability, and fast."

"Unreliable?"

My husband's intense gaze held mine captive. "Your visit to the meth lab yesterday was probably the straw that broke the camel's back."

I blanched. "You're saying I got Jakie killed?"

"His drug use and the paranoia and bad decisions that went along with it got him killed. Normal's backwoods business acumen and his ability to cut his losses — however extreme that might be — got Jakie killed. But you may have been the catalyst in an already volatile situation."

The coffee sliding down my throat was tepid, but the acid roiling in my stomach felt hot as Hades.

"If Jakie had just come to the door when you knocked and said you had the wrong house, everything might have been fine. At least for a while. But he went a little bonkers."

"I'll say. Is there any possibility Normal could know you guys are watching him?"

He didn't look surprised at the question, which surprised me. "It's possible. He's got the survival instincts of a cockroach. Why?"

I told him about Normal yelling at Jakie as I was getting ready to drive away from the house. "I remember the words 'cop,' and 'wife.' So he knows more about either you or me or both of us than he ought to."

"Great." I hadn't thought Barr could sound any more tired, but he could. Did.

"I need to get on the horn and call some people, let them know," he said. "Normal could very well be getting ready to scamper."

He pulled his phone out of his pocket and pushed back his chair. I heard him murmuring in the living room. Half his breakfast remained on his plate.

I picked up his fork and took a few mouthfuls, hoping the solid food would help settle my stomach. It seemed ages since last night's spaghetti dinner.

When I heard him say goodbye, I carried his coffee out to the living room. He was looking through my book on poisonous plants.

"Thanks," he said as I handed him the cup for the second time that morning. "I've got a couple hours before I need to be back. The commander's stepping things up regarding Normal, but he told me to take a shower, maybe get in a nap."

"Well, at least he's letting you do that," I said.

"You know, I don't like how much this drug case is siphoning attention and resources away from the investigation into Quentin Swenson's death."

"Murder," I corrected, not mentioning that he hadn't been so excited about preventing Quentin's death in the first place. But that was probably unfair. He'd had valid reasons for focusing on the cases he already had.

"Presumably, though we need the official tox report to confirm. But yes — murder."

"Is Robin spending all her time on the drug case, too?"

A crooked grin flashed across his face. "On the drug case and on the state patrol's lieutenant liaison."

"Oooh."

"She's making noises about applying for a crime scene investigation position with the state laboratory. They deal with drug labs all the time, and apparently she's having a ball with this."

"And with the lieutenant."

"Him, too."

"Where would Normal go if he left?" I asked, changing the subject.

"I don't know. He's lived here his whole life. You know what really chaps my butt about this case?"

I smiled and shook my head.

"It started out being about marijuana. Lots and lots of it suddenly available in town. Then the pot became less available, and the meth increased. Like one was taking over for the other. At first we thought it was supply and demand. But now the marijuana consumption is starting to increase again."

I thought for a long moment. "Like maybe it's more a case of supply and supply."

He pointed a finger at me. "That's what I don't get. It's like the pot conduit dried up, and Normal replaced it with meth to make up for his lack of profits. But he hasn't been doing it for that long, so the local damage is still relatively low. We want to stop it before we have a real problem on our hands. Then the pot conduit opens again, and we've got both to deal with. He's created a strong starter market for the meth."

The blood drained from my face. "Barr — how strong are we talking about? Are there meth addicts at the high school?"

"A few, according to the kids who are our sources, but so far they're more interested in drinking and smoking pot. The meth seems to be filtering into a slightly older population."

I wondered whether Normal had anything to do with that. Wasn't he concerned about getting kids hooked on something as serious as methamphetamine? Then I mentally slapped my forehead with my palm. Duh. Barr said the guy had killed Jakie. What was I thinking? Normal Brown obviously didn't care who he hurt.

"So I wonder what happened to the marijuana supply," Barr said, looking out the window at the sun trying valiantly to break through the early morning clouds.

"Dang it," I said, struggling to remember. Barr looked the question at me.

"The first time I went to the meadery with

Erin, I overheard something. Dorothy was telling Normal he couldn't do something he'd been doing. She'd made other arrangements. He said he hadn't, though. She seemed fine with that."

His narrowed eyes were almost a glare. "First off, how did you happen to hear a conversation like that?"

"I, er —"

"She snuck down a hallway and listened outside their office," Erin said from the doorway. She yawned high and wide, remembering belatedly to cover her mouth. She wore white pajamas with blue stars on them that made her look eight years old.

"There's stuff to eat in the kitchen," I said quickly.

She didn't budge.

Barr didn't say anything, but his glare deepened. Then he rubbed his fingers across his unshaven chin and said, "What *exactly* did you overhear at the meadery?"

I threw up my hands. "A few seconds after that I was scared half out of my wits by the recently deceased, unnormal Normal, and the Dorothy and Cabot show. I can't give you anything verbatim, just the idea I got that Normal had been involved with something at the meadery and Dorothy had cut him off."

"They saw you? So you've had contact with both Normal and Jakie more than once."

"I didn't mean to. How did I know they'd even be at the meadery? They're not involved with the place in any way, from what I've been told."

He sighed. "Just like you didn't expect them to be at the rundown, piece-of-crap house you thought Iris lived in."

"Hey!" I already felt pretty stupid about that.

"No wonder Jakie got upset when you showed up on his doorstep," Barr said, leaning forward.

Erin took a couple of steps forward. "I can tell you what they said. I wrote it all down." She turned and ran down the hall to her bedroom.

TWENTY-SEVEN

" 'Stop asking. We've made other arrangements for shipping to Canada.' " Erin read in a stilted monotone. She looked up. "I don't know if I got the very beginning or not. You were already down the hallway by the time I got out of the restroom."

"You found me very quickly." Meghan would not be pleased.

"I figured you'd be snooping somewhere."

Barr's low sigh was barely audible.

"I'm sure that was Dorothy speaking," I said.

Erin nodded. "It was a woman." She continued to read from her notebook. " 'You don't understand. I haven't been able to make other arrangements.' "

"Normal?" Barr asked.

I nodded. "Go on, Bug."

" 'Good. You need to stop that foolishness and simply stick to your other activities. Aren't they sketchy enough? I swear, Normal, I live in fear that someone will find out about all that nonsense. Do you even realize the position you could put this business in? Or do you simply not care?' And then a man again. 'Ah, Sis.' Then the lady," Erin said, getting into the dialog and changing the timbre of her voice. She had a knack for the dramatic. " 'Don't you 'ah, Sis' me, old man.' "

Now her voice went low. " 'He should be the one running this outfit, anyway. He loaned you the seed money to start this place. And now you've got the nerve to tell us we can't be part of the Canada runs?' "

"That last bit was Jakie," I said, vibrating with revulsion. Erin's newfound instinct for voices extended even to Gigantor.

"And then the other lady yelled to stay away from a chair and they all came out into the hallway."

Barr's lips pressed together, but he didn't comment.

"The other lady was Cabot, the assistant. She was pushing Dorothy's wheelchair."

"Bug," he said. "Would you do me a humongous favor?"

She nodded her enthusiasm. "Sure."

"It would really help me out if you'd write the stuff you just read to us down on another piece of paper for me to take to work."

"It's in my computer. I'll print it out."

"Perfect."

"Did I help?"

He got up and walked to her. Hugged her against his waist. "You sure did."

She scurried back to her room to do his bidding. He returned to the sofa.

"Did that mean anything to you?" I asked.

"It does." The gloom that had dominated his mood since coming home that morning had lifted. "I believe it confirms that Normal was using Grendel's delivery trucks to bring marijuana in from Canada. Dorothy caught wind of it and nixed the whole deal. That's when he started up the meth lab."

"But what about the new influx of pot in the area?"

"One, there could be a new player in town. Or two, Normal found a way around his sister that she doesn't even know about yet."

"Then why was he trying to get her to let him go back to whatever he was doing before?"

"If he didn't protest, she might get suspicious, don't you think?"

I pointed my finger at him. "You're right. But what about the new system? Do you think it still involves the meadery?"

"I'd bet on it," Barr said.

"Wouldn't that be a little risky?"

"Hon, the whole shebang is risky. But I'm guessing his new setup isn't as secure as the one his sister stopped."

"So Dorothy knew all about Normal's antics," I mused. "And so did Cabot. In fact, I bet she knew most of the things Dorothy did — about Glenwood's business failings, for example, and the lawsuit against Quentin."

Barr closed his eyes and leaned his head back on the sofa cushion.

"Say, what's her first name?" I asked. "I haven't heard anyone call her anything but Cabot."

Eyes still closed he said, "That is her first name."

"Really? Who names their child Cabot, for heaven's sake? What did they call her when she was five? Cabbie?"

One side of his mouth turned up. "I've only met her once, but I'm pretty sure she's not the sort of woman who has a nickname — certainly not one like that."

I snorted. "You're right. So what's her last name?"

"Reyes."

"And what was Jakie's last name? Don't

285

tell me Jakie was his last name."

"Nope. It was Owens."

"Jakie Owens and Cabot Reyes. Sounds like a couple of short stops."

A small snore escaped Barr's throat. Since he was sitting up like that, I wasn't surprised. I made my way over and cleared the pile of books from the sofa beside him. Laid a pillow on the end and started to ease him over. He woke with a start, realized what I was doing, and settled into a horizontal position.

As I tucked an afghan around him, he mumbled, "Wake me in an hour."

I scrambled fresh eggs for Erin and heated up the potatoes and bacon. When I left her to go upstairs and take a shower, she had a piece of bacon hanging out of the corner of her mouth and was doodling pictures in the now infamous red notebook.

I reveled in the hot water splashing across my bare shoulders. After receiving copious amounts of arnica salve, my ankle seemed to be improving already. The bruise had already gone from purple to mottled purple and yellow, and the swelling had decreased despite working most of the night and getting only an hour's worth of sleep. Turning the water a notch hotter and inhaling the steam, I shampooed my hair and reflected on how resilient the human body was.

Unless someone shot you in the chest, of course.

Jakie was dead. Barr thought Normal did it. That felt like pretty straightforward police work to me. Physical evidence and all that. Clean and fairly simple to prove one way or the other.

But what about Quentin? And Elizabeth? Barr had said himself he hadn't been able to focus on that investigation as much as he'd like. And his partner, Detective Lane, might not even be on the Cadyville force much longer.

Sheesh.

Too bad none of my earlier ruminations, in bed or in my ducky slippers, had brought clarity to what I more and more considered "my" case.

I inhaled deeply of the Winding Road Wake Up soap I'd developed for early mornings. The essential oil blend was the same as for the bath melts I'd made earlier in the week: equal parts rosemary, eucalyptus, tea tree, and peppermint. A few whiffs of that and my brain kicked into overdrive.

Wait a minute. Reyes? *Cabot Reyes?*

Holy cow. I'd been going at this from the wrong direction.

■ ■ ■ ■

"Wake up." I shook Barr's shoulder. "You said an hour. It's eight thirty."

"Mmmph." He grabbed me and pulled me down to him. Nuzzled my neck. "You smell good."

I giggled. I hate it when I giggle, but I'm horribly ticklish, and his scratchy beard was too much. Then he gave me a gentle little nip, and I squealed.

I hate it when I squeal.

Pushing him away, I said, "Well, you smell like a goat. Personally, I have nothing against goats. I rather like them. But I think you'd better shower before meeting up with your police-y cohorts."

"Fine." He swung his feet to the floor and stood.

I did, too, immediately shifting weight from my ankle and trying not to wince. Improved, yes. All better, no.

Erin was outside feeding the chickens, making sure they had fresh water and plenty of oyster shell to peck at. After gathering the morning eggs, she'd offered to weed one of the raised garden beds. I would have thought it entirely altruistic but knew in truth she thought of it as harvesting treats for the hens. Their fondness for chickweed and the like accounted for the deep orangey yellow of the yolks in their eggs.

So I followed Barr upstairs and made the bed while he scrubbed and shaved in the shower. I dusted and picked up the bedroom, and made a quick pass through our sitting room and the kitchenette off the office area that we pretty much used for bills and personal correspondence. I preferred to keep Winding Road paperwork confined to the storeroom, and Barr liked to work on his laptop while sitting in bed.

Should I tell him what I was thinking about Cabot Reyes?

He came into the bedroom and dressed in clean clothes as I was separating the dirty ones in the hamper to wash. He still looked tired, but the nap and shower had obviously refreshed him.

"Remember when I told you about the file box that was missing from Elizabeth's office?" I asked, tossing a T-shirt onto the pile of darks.

He grabbed his favorite silver steer's head string tie and snugged it up under the collar of a light blue shirt. "Uh-huh."

"It contained the letters Q through S."

He stopped and looked at me, waiting for the punch line.

"And Cabot's name is Reyes."

His eyebrows slowly rose. "So it is."

"And Elizabeth never actually said on the tape that her client was a Swenson. She only said that she was going to warn the others in the Swenson family against one of their own. Don't you think Nurse Reyes would qualify as one of their own?"

Barr perched on the side of the freshly made bed. "Why would Cabot want to kill Quentin? Isn't it a lot more likely that Victoria was seeing Elizabeth on the sly about her addiction to pain medication? At least she has a monetary motive to kill her brother."

"True . . ." I said.

"And according to your own photographs — did you e-mail those to me? Thanks. Anyway, she's growing the poison hemlock that probably killed her brother. Damn it," he exclaimed. "I need to get the warrant for the meadery garden this morning and get that tea over to the lab, too. Hon, I've got to go."

I waved my hand. "Go. And don't forget the warrant for the mead at Elizabeth's house."

"Things won't be this crazy for much longer," he said. "We'll get everything sorted out and back to normal."

"I know. At least Meghan is coming home this morning."

He kissed me, grabbed his briefcase, and went downstairs. I followed at a more leisurely — and less painful — pace.

TWENTY-EIGHT

I rubbed more arnica salve into my ankle, then tidied up after Erin's KP duty. Wiping down the counters and putting the raspberry jam back in the fridge on autopilot, I thought about what Barr had said.

I wasn't convinced Victoria had killed her brother. Her grief had been quietly evident at the family meeting at Willa's house. Maybe I was wrong, though. Perhaps she was an excellent actress.

Cabot, on the other hand, hadn't seemed all that upset about Quentin's death. Of course, he wasn't her brother, either. And I wouldn't have been surprised if she'd learned over the years to keep her feelings regarding her employer's family to herself. She'd oozed distanced professionalism every time I'd seen her.

But she had just as much opportunity and ability as Victoria to kill Quentin. She was at the meadery with Dorothy nearly every day. She knew all the ins and outs of the place, and after fifteen years was bound to know as much about mead making and Grendel's business affairs as any of the Swensons. She was a nurse, too. It was quite possible she knew a thing or two about plant-based poisons. She and Dorothy had both been in the garden the previous morning. Dorothy's nurse companion had free run of the place. She was almost like a member of the family.

And surely she got a break from Dorothy once in awhile. A day off. Time alone, time to run errands, shop, have a bit of a life.

Time to go to a therapist. To brew up a batch of poison hemlock. To spike a bottle of mead and reseal it with a shrink-wrap band.

But Barr was right about Cabot's lack of obvious motive. Maybe there was something a bit less obvious though. I reached for the phone.

Tootie picked up on the second ring.

"It's Sophie Mae. I'm sorry to call so early," I said by way of greeting. After all, Emily Post said phone calls before the hour of nine a.m. were rude.

"Nonsense. We're early risers around here."

I heard a voice in the background. Felix

already there in her room, probably to take her down the hall to the dining room. Only . . . she'd said, "We're early risers." Maybe Felix was *still* there. Did Caladia Acres allow sleepovers between residents?

That thought hurt my brain, so I hurried on. "Last night you said Dorothy talked about her will with some of the people there at Caladia Acres."

"I didn't mean to make it sound like she was bragging about her money. Wills tend to naturally crop up in conversation in a place like this, where our happy hunting grounds are just around the corner."

A sound of protest from Felix.

"Oh, now, you know I'm right," she said, apparently to him. "We talk about things here that simply aren't discussed out in the real world. Like that whole conversation Edna and Ruby had the other day about laxatives."

"Ahem," I said.

"Sorry, dear." Tootie spoke back into the telephone handset.

"I'm not worried about whether Dorothy bragged about her money or not," I said. "I was wondering whether she had ever mentioned leaving anything to Cabot Reyes."

"Reyes? I thought Cabot was her last name."

294

That made me feel a bit less stupid. "Me, too."

"Well, Dorothy never said anything to me about it, but hang on, and I'll check with Felix." Indecipherable murmurs for a few moments, and then she came back on the line.

"He says Dorothy did allude to Cabot being taken care of after she was gone."

"Do you know if Dorothy was going to leave her a share equal to the grandkids'?"

More murmurs.

"Felix doesn't know," she said. "Hang on. He wants to talk to you."

"Sophie Mae?"

"Hi, Felix."

"How are you, darlin'?" He barreled on without waiting for an answer. "I don't know about the share that Cabot gal will get when ol' Dorothy kicks off, but they're supposed to be here for lunch today. Do you want me to try and find out?"

"No! I mean, thank you, but I don't want her nurse to know I'm asking about the will."

"Okey dokey."

"But Felix? When Dorothy said that about taking care of Cabot, did she say it in front of her?"

"Hmm. I don't recall . . . nope, I'm pretty

sure the big one had gone to get Dorothy a cup of tea or something. She runs that gal around pretty good, you know."

We said goodbye. I gimped my way down-stairs to get the UPS *Pick Up* sign. Brodie waddled out and lifted a leg when I attached the sign to the front fence, then we both toddled back inside. I wrapped up the few oatmeal molasses cookies Erin hadn't eaten yet and put them outside the basement door with the boxes I'd loaded in the middle of the night. As long as UPS Joe was willing to go around to the alley to pick up the boxes so I didn't have to lug them upstairs, I was happy to provide him with sweet treats.

All the while, my mind gnawed at the no-tion of Cabot as murderer. If she did get an equal portion of Dorothy's estate, then her motive would be the same as any of the other siblings: fewer pieces of the money pie equaled bigger pieces for those left. But what if she didn't? Well, she was a nurse, and Quentin had been a pharmacist. Maybe there was some kind of connection there.

Great. A whole new drug connection.

Or not.

Back in my storeroom, I tidied items on the shelves and tried to decide what I still needed to make more of. I'd shipped many orders out to the natural food store chain but still had several more to fill. I had to get rid of Penny, and quick, so I could get some real help. I was too old to pull any more all-nighters.

I yawned.

The last time I'd seen Cabot, she'd been in the herb garden. But she'd also been at the family meeting at Willa's house after Quentin died. She knew I'd tried to warn Willa, and that Willa had told others in the family. She knew I was interested in how Quentin died and suspected foul play. She'd known everything Dorothy had. She was involved with the family and the family business more than Quentin himself had been.

And she'd told me how to get to Iris's house. I sank into my desk chair as I considered that. Naturally, I'd assumed my horrible sense of direction had been responsible for ending up at Normal's meth lab. Now I wasn't so sure.

What if Cabot had sent me there on purpose? What if she knew Jakie and Normal were manufacturing methamphetamine? Which then begged the question of whether Dorothy knew about that aspect of her brother's illegal conduct.

But why would Cabot send me to a drug lab? Did she think it would distract me from

Quentin's death? To throw me off her trail? Because frankly, I hadn't been on her trail.

Or did she intend for Jakie to hurt me, or worse? Everyone — even good old Felix — knew Jakie was dangerous. Perhaps she'd hoped he would take care of me, and she wouldn't have to.

Well. That just made me mad.

"Sophie Mae? Where are you?" Erin called from the kitchen.

"Down in the basement."

Her footsteps clattered down the wooden steps, and moments later her elfin face popped around the edge of the door frame. "Whatcha doin'?"

"Trying to figure out how I'm going to get all my work done."

"When's Mom getting home?"

I looked at my watch. "A couple hours."

"I'm going to take these eggs over to Mrs. Gray, then."

"Say hi to her from me."

Erin left by my workroom door. I watched her cross the alley and go into Mavis Gray's backyard. Four more dollars in her pocket. I wondered how much money she'd squirreled away since the hens had started laying.

So, still thinking hypothetically, once Cabot poisoned the mead that Quentin —

and probably Elizabeth — drank, how did she get them to drink it?

I pulled up Elizabeth's website on my computer. Her freckled face smiled out at me as I called Barr. He actually answered his cell.

"Hey, it's me. Did you get the warrants?" I asked.

"The one for the meadery, yes. The toxicology report came back positive for poison hemlock in Quentin's system. The pictures you took at the meadery helped, and I don't know if you noticed, but I also borrowed that book on poisonous plants. The judge signed off on it right away."

"How about the other one?"

"There's no certain link between Moser and Quentin Swenson. Even though I played the tape, the judge was on the fence. See, while the letters and numbers on the tapes seem to indicate dates, there's no proof that it's actually Elizabeth Moser speaking."

I stared at Elizabeth's face as we spoke. Her voice and words were as clear in my mind as the first time I'd heard them. Who else would be saying those things about clients?

"So I took the tape to the lab when I dropped off Victoria's tea for analysis," Barr said. "They'll determine whether or not the recording has been altered, and then we can have a friend or relative identify the voice."

"But the tape would still be hearsay," I said.

"Right. Since Moser didn't record the actual client session, and we don't hear the client threaten a member of the Swenson family. We only hear the therapist relate what the client said. But we're only talking about a warrant here, not an indictment. It should be enough to get us in the door now that Quentin Swenson's death is a definite homicide. Especially since he died in much the same way Elizabeth Moser did."

My brain hurt as I tried to wrap it around the technicalities. "How long will it take?"

"Depends on how quickly the lab works and how fast we can get an identification." His voice lowered to a murmur. "Listen, I have to go now. The team is interrogating Grendel delivery drivers today, trying to figure out how Normal used the trucks to move marijuana. Wish us luck."

"Good luck, Detective Ambrose. I hope you nail the old son of a —"

The door to the alley opened.

"Well, anyway — good luck."

Erin came in as I was hanging up. "She sure does talk a lot."

I laughed. "Mrs. Gray is very social, is all."

She waved a five dollar bill. "She tipped me."

"Bug —"

"Said it was for delivering the eggs to her door."

But I was distracted. The more I thought about that mead in Elizabeth's closet, the more I wanted to make sure it was still there. Mrs. Deveaux had said the sister from Yakima had been coming up on the week-ends, and today was Saturday. There wasn't a lot left in the house; what if she planned to clear it all out?

Upstairs, the front door opened and Meghan called, "Anybody home?"

"Mom!" Erin flew up the steps.

I found mother and daughter hugging in the foyer. With their dark curls and slight builds they looked like clones.

Shuffling to join them, I said, "Welcome back! You're early."

"Caught an earlier flight out of Chicago." Meghan's gray eyes narrowed over Erin's shoulder. "What happened to your foot?"

"Sophie Mae sprained her ankle," Erin answered for me. "Running away from a big scary guy."

Meghan opened her mouth, but I cut her

off. "And how do you know that?" I asked Erin.

Her eyes opened wide, and she bit her bottom lip.

I glanced up at Meghan then back at her daughter, who looked the picture of innocence. "In fact, there are a lot of things you seem to know that maybe you shouldn't."

Blink blink.

Meghan smiled.

I didn't. "Spill, you little imp."

She stubbed her toe into the ground. "Mom . . ."

"Sounds to me like you have something to explain," Meghan said, arching one perfect eyebrow.

Erin's sigh was long-winded and dramatic. "Heater vent."

"What?"

"I can hear you talk in your bedroom through the heater vent. Always could. It's just that you didn't used to talk much when you were up there by yourself. And when you did, it wasn't very interesting."

Meghan tried to stifle a laugh.

Oh, good God. I closed my eyes and covered them with my hand. What all had she heard? Had she sneaked out of her bedroom and listened when we thought she was asleep? Here I was all worried about her hearing something inappropriate in Elizabeth Moser's notes, and for all I knew she'd listened to Barr and me having sex.

Not that we were that loud. Usually.

Welcome home, Meghan.

I lowered my hand to my mouth and met my housemate's gaze. She started to giggle.

Erin joined her. Such camaraderie between the generations.

"You really think it's funny?" I asked.

Meghan sobered. "Might as well. Can't do anything about it now. But maybe we should soundproof that vent somehow. In the meantime, young lady . . ." She looked down at her daughter's upturned face. "You are expressly forbidden to listen at that vent. If you do, there will be some real trouble in it for you."

Erin pouted but nodded her agreement.

TWENTY-NINE

While Meghan hauled her luggage in with Erin's help, I went upstairs and dug a pair of loose sandals out of the closet. I'd been wearing my ducky slippers around the house, but now I needed something suitable for public consumption.

Back in the foyer, Erin was tearing the wrapping off a box. She pulled out a bag of salt water taffy from New Jersey.

"Cool! What else did you get me?"

"Don't get greedy," Meghan said. "I'm saving the rest for your birthday tomorrow."

"I guess I can wait."

"Put those in the kitchen. You're not eating them all at once."

"Okay." The word was mangled by the piece of taffy already in her mouth.

"I need to borrow your car," I said, gathering my tote bag and holding out my hand for the keys. "Erin can help you unpack, and you guys can catch up."

Meghan's eyebrows knotted. "Where do you need to be in such an all-fired hurry? And why do you need to drive my car?"

"I bet she's going to go investigate another murder," Erin crowed, happy to out me.

My housemate's shoulders dropped, "oh, no" all over her face.

"Your car is an automatic, so I can drive it with my bum ankle. I'm just going over to look at someone's fiber stash." It wasn't exactly a lie, merely a little truth-fudging.

Unsuccessful, though, because Meghan shook her head. "You're not taking time out in the middle of the day for that. I could tell something was going on while I was gone." She dropped the keys in my hand. "Be careful of your ankle. And don't get hurt."

I gave her another quick hug. "Thanks."

As I limped out the door I heard her say, "Well, Bug, since you seem to know everything, you might as well fill me in."

Not sure which house Mrs. Deveaux lived in, I parked in front of Elizabeth's, got out and stood in the middle of the sidewalk. It took nearly a minute for her to come out of the house on the right. Her short gray hair was even wilder than the last time I'd seen her.

"Hello," I said.

"Mrs. Ambrose." Sharp eyes flashed behind the tortoiseshell frames.

"Do you happen to know if Elizabeth's sister has disposed of the rest of her things?"

Her head inclined a fraction. "Some of them."

"I suppose I should call her directly."

"No need. She's inside." And with that, Mrs. Charles Deveaux stomped back into her own house.

Elizabeth's front door was open a crack, and swung open at my touch. Voices drifted out from the rear bedroom.

"Hello?"

Ruth Black's head popped around the door frame. "Sophie Mae! Come on in. Did you change your mind?"

"Change my mind about what?"

I followed her into the room I'd seen through the window and found the floor strewn with all manner of yarns and roving, silk "handkerchiefs" ready to spin, and a big blue vase with an elaborate bouquet of drop spindles jutting out of it.

"About taking some of this lovely wool and cotton off of Jenna's hands. Jenna Moser, this is Sophie Mae Ambrose. She's the one who gave me your phone number."

Jenna looked an awful lot like the picture

of Elizabeth Moser on her website. Deep frown lines at the sides of her mouth and smaller eyes, but definitely her sister.

"Hi," I said.

Her head bobbed once, like a robin plucking a worm from the ground. "You were a friend of Elizabeth's? I confess, I never understood her silly fascination with making yarn when you can simply buy it."

I glanced at Ruth, who was carefully avoiding my eye. "I'm afraid I never met your sister."

Jenna frowned.

"Her neighbor happened to tell me you wanted to find someone to take this stuff, and I immediately thought of Ruth."

"One woman's junk is another woman's treasure," Ruth said.

The bottles of mead were still on the shelf in the closet.

I continued. "The same neighbor told me you were in here. When do you think the house will go on the market?"

Jenna gave me a knowing wink. "So that's it. You're interested in the house."

"Maybe," I said.

Ruth's head whipped around, but she stayed quiet.

"The realtor is listing it the first of the week. If you want to get a jump on the competition, give me your name now, and I'll give you first right of refusal."

"Let me think about it," I said, already thinking hard.

The mead would likely be gone by the end of the day. Not only was it possibly the only evidence that Elizabeth had been murdered, but it could be downright dangerous. But I couldn't just take it out of the house.

Or could I? I made a decision.

"Oh, look." I pointed. "Mead. I love mead."

"What is it?" Jenna asked, craning her head to read the label.

"Honey wine. I'll be happy to take this off your hands. I'll pay you, of course."

Ruth watched me. I could tell she knew something was up, but she didn't say anything.

Jenna fluttered her fingers dismissively. "Just take them."

Maybe she was trying to get on the good side of a potential home buyer, but I didn't care. I carefully lifted each bottle with my fingertips and put them in my tote bag.

"Sophie Mae," Ruth said. "Did you notice that one of the bottles has been opened?"

I gave her a hard look then peered inside my tote. "I believe you're mistaken, Ruth."

Her eyebrows raised three millimeters but

she didn't protest, willing to play along for now. Bless her heart.

"Okay, then. I just thought I'd drop by and see how things are going. Places to go and things to do now, though. Nice to meet you, Jenna." I waved and sailed out the door, slowing to my recent halting limp as soon as I hit the living room.

Ruth came up behind me and put her hand under my elbow, echoing the way I supported Tootie when we walked together. "You are going to tell me what that was all about," she said once we were on the front walk.

"The whole story," I said. "Later. I promise."

"All right, then." She let go of my arm, and I got into Meghan's Volvo. "I'll look forward to it."

I drove to the police station, steeling myself for a reprimand. I'd no doubt screwed up the chain of evidence on the mead, though that might be mitigated by Ruth as my witness. What choice did I have, though? Barr couldn't get a search warrant before Jenna Moser threw the mead away — or worse, drank it. I'd considered telling her the whole story, but it seemed cruel to bring up the idea of her sister being murdered until there was some hard evidence to back me up. And even if I had told her the story, would it have changed the provenance of the honey wine? Should I have forced her to bring the mead to the station herself? Would she have?

Too many nights with too little sleep. I couldn't trust whether I'd made the right call or not.

At least I'd handled the bottles very carefully, so the authorities could recover any fingerprints. Which might be a moot point because Elizabeth had been cremated and didn't have any fingerprints anymore. Or fingers. But maybe she was in the system someplace. I could always hope.

Barr wasn't at the station. The multijurisdictional team must have been questioning truck drivers at another facility. I didn't ask the cadet at the front counter, though, because I probably wasn't supposed to know anything about the drug investigation.

Great. Now what?

"Sophie Mae?"

I turned to find my husband's partner, Detective Robin Lane, coming in the door. A state trooper followed close on her heels.

"Thank God," I said. "I need a favor."

She tossed her gorgeous mane of dark red hair. "I thought your husband was the guy you went to for favors."

No need to be snotty. "He's not here. I need you to log in two pieces of potential evidence."

That got her attention. "Evidence of what?"

"Of murder. You're working with him on the Swenson homicide, aren't you?"

"Of course."

"And you found a bottle of mead next to Quentin's body, which later contained poison hemlock, right?"

Her face screwed up. "You sure seem to know an awful lot about the case."

I ignored her. "Well, these —" I pulled the bottles of mead out of my tote bag and set them on the counter. "— may also contain poison hemlock. In fact, Barr tried to get a search warrant for them this morning."

"So how do you happen to have them?" she asked, petite nostrils flaring.

"I asked the owner for them. She gave them to me. In front of a witness. And I brought them straight here."

The state trooper had been listening in silence. Now she turned to him. Her voice took on a sexy undertone. "Give me a minute?"

"Sure." He said the word like it was an intimate sweet nothing.

Oh, brother.

She tipped her head to one side and considered me. "Why didn't you wait for the warrant to come through?"

"Because the judge wanted more evidence. Because the woman I think this stuff killed has a sister who was clearing out her house. If it's evidence I didn't want to lose it altogether, and I didn't want anyone to get hurt if it contains a toxic substance."

She dialed her phone. "Barr, your wife is here. I think you should talk to her." She handed her phone to me and said, "I'll go get a couple evidence bags."

THIRTY

Robin agreed to take the mead to the crime lab. She wasn't even cranky about it, a fact I put down to her recently falling in love. Give it three or four months and the old difficult Detective Lane would be back on the prowl.

I just hoped she continued to prowl in Cadyville. She wasn't the easiest person to take, but she was smart and effective. Barr and she had ironed out the kinks in their working relationship, and breaking in a new partner all over again would be a pain.

Speaking of new partners, Penny had left a message on my voicemail saying she wouldn't be able to come to work that afternoon. Something about a spur-of-the-moment, Saturday afternoon barbecue. She was kind enough to invite me to attend, though.

All my worries about letting her go vanished with that message. In fact, I wasn't going to wait one more second. Even though I rarely talked on my phone in the car, I hit the callback button as I drove. Five rings later, she picked up.

"Hi, Sophie Mae! Will you be able to make our little party?"

"I'm afraid not," I said through gritted teeth. "See, Penny, I have a business to run. I have orders to fill."

"But it's Saturday."

"Not in my world. In my world there are no Saturdays until the work is done, and then that Saturday may come on a Tuesday."

Silence on the other end of the line.

"Penny, I'm very sorry, but I'm afraid we're going to have to revisit our arrangement." I chose my words carefully. "It's not really working out that well for you, is it?"

I heard a big whoosh of air. "Oh, honey, you are so clever to see that. I just didn't know how to tell you, but I don't have as much time as I thought I did."

No kidding.

"Well, let's go ahead and cancel your work schedule. That'll free you up for the important things in your life." Like tending to your adult son's every whim.

"That is so sweet of you to understand," she said, completely missing my sarcasm.

Just as well. Hiring Penny had been

enough of a fiasco. No need to burn bridges.

"You enjoy your barbecue now," I said.

"You're sure you can't come?"

"Positive. Thanks anyway. I'll send you a check for the time you put in this past week."

As I severed the connection with my erstwhile employee, I pulled into a parking spot across the street from the Blackwell Building. Still in the car, I speed-dialed Cyan Waters' number.

She picked right up. "Hey, Sophie Mae."

"Hey. How was prom?"

"Like, awesome."

"Like, excellent."

"Did you need me to come in today?"

Now *that* was an employee.

"Haven't you been up all night?"

"Just until three or so."

Yeah. Me, too.

"Well, if you want to come in and make some extra money, you sure can. But you don't have to. It's the day after prom, for heaven's sake. Actually, I called to see if you have any friends as amazing as you. I'm looking to hire another employee."

"Penny's gone, huh?"

"How did you know?"

"You could just tell she wasn't that into it. Um, my friend Kendra is working at Mc-

315

Donalds, and she hates it, so she might be interested. She's a hard worker. I'll ask her."

"I'll still have to interview her, of course."

"Duh."

I laughed. Why had I ever thought Penny would be more responsible than Cyan just because she was older? Cyan had never been anything but punctual and efficient, and the year before she'd kept Winding Road going by herself when I'd gone to Colorado to look into my brother's suicide.

"I'm promoting you to assistant manager," I said.

"Cool. How much more money do I get?"

Bonnie Parr's face lit up when I entered the room, then fell when she realized I wasn't one of her doctors' clients. I grabbed a chair, carried it to her massive reception desk, and made myself comfortable.

"Ms. Ambrose," she said, the stud in her nose winking in the light from the window.

"Bonnie, I need you to check Elizabeth Moser's client list for me again."

This request did not appear to bring her joy.

"Please," I tried.

"I don't —"

"You see, Quentin Swenson is dead now."

She blinked wide eyes.

I went on. "I was trying to save someone when I came in here before and asked all those questions about Elizabeth. I just didn't know who. It turned out to be Quentin, and he might not be the only one." That sounded suitably dramatic. Unfortunately, it was the God's honest truth. "So are you going to help me?"

Her gaze shot to Dr. Simms' closed door.

"He said it was okay once. I can't imagine that's changed."

Bonnie's shoulders slumped. Digging around in a lower desk drawer, she asked, "What's the name?"

"Reyes." If Cabot's name wasn't on Elizabeth's client list, we were back to all the circumstantial evidence against Victoria Swenson.

But Bonnie stopped rummaging and sat up in her chair again. "Cabot Reyes?"

Bingo!

I resisted the urge to leap to my feet and do a little dance. Instead, I acted like the grownup I was and merely nodded. "So you knew her."

Puzzlement wavered across her face. "She came in a few times during the day, but she was one of Moser's after-hours patients most of the time. The thing is —" she hesitated, and her brow wrinkled.

"What?" I prompted.

"Someone else just called and wanted to know if Reyes was one of Elizabeth's clients."

I felt the skin tighten across my face in surprise. "Who?"

"She sounded old. Said her name was Dorothy."

Oh, dear. My mind raced. Not good. Not good at all.

"What did you tell her?"

"I said I couldn't give that kind of information out over the phone. That I'd need the approval of one of the doctors even if she came in."

"So you didn't confirm it."

"Well . . . no."

I stood and leaned over the desk. "Did you tell her or not?"

Her head jerked back. "You don't have to yell."

Deep breath. "I'm sorry. Did you tell her or not?"

Bonnie looked pretty miserable as she said, "No. But she said she could tell from my voice."

"Damn."

Willa had said her grandmother lived two blocks away, but I didn't know the exact address. She'd been listed under Swenson the first time I'd looked the name up, though.

"Let me see your phone book."

Silent, Bonnie opened a drawer and handed me the slim volume.

"Swenson, Swenson. There she is." I ripped out the whole page. "Thanks." And I ran out of there as fast as my little ankle could carry me.

On the sidewalk, I called the Grendel Meadery and asked the breathy young voice who answered if I could speak with Dorothy Swenson.

"I'm sorry. Ms. Swenson is out ill today. May I take a message?"

"Thank you. No message."

Out ill.

More like home alone with a killer.

THIRTY-ONE

I speed-dialed Barr's cell phone. Again.

Pick up, pick up, pick up.

His hello sounded an awful lot like, "What now?"

I loped across the street toward the Volvo. "Meet me over at Dorothy Swenson's house."

A pause, then, "What's going on?"

"I know who killed Quentin, and probably Elizabeth as well." The key slid into the lock. I climbed in and started the engine.

"Dorothy Swenson? You've got to be kidding."

"No, no. Not Dorothy. Nurse Reyes. I just checked with the receptionist at the Blackwell Healing Center. She confirmed that Cabot was one of Elizabeth Moser's clients. That's who she was talking about on the tape. Her file was among those stolen from the office after Elizabeth died. I was right. It wasn't about getting the 'S' files at all."

"Hang on a minute. So Moser's reception-ist said Reyes was a client. Did she —"

"I wasn't the only one asking about Cabot. Dorothy called, too. Listen, I promise to explain it all later. Just trust me on this."

"I'm going to need all the details if I'm going to get a warrant and —"

"No time, Barr. Meet me over there. She lives two blocks from Willa." I rattled off the address.

"Sophie Mae —"

"Please, *please* trust me. Cabot killed Quentin, and Dorothy knows that. I'm afraid she could be in real danger. There's no telling what Cabot might do to that old lady. We've got to get over there."

"Shit," he said. "I'm on my way, but I'm on the far edge of town. Wait for me. Do not — I repeat — *do not* go into that house."

"Don't worry, I won't. I promise."

I drove a couple hundred yards past the Swenson matriarch's house and parked across the street. Painted dove-gray and boasting cedar shakes, it was the largest home on the block. The curtains were open on the second floor, but were drawn across the windows on the first floor. Strange for the middle of the day. Made me think about Normal and Jakie's meth lab in the woods.

Something wasn't right.

Twitchy and nervous, I got out of the car and stood on the sidewalk. Could she see me? Maybe I should have parked farther down.

Where was Barr? He'd said he was on the far edge of town, but Cadyville was hardly big enough to have a far edge. He should have been here by now.

The edge of the curtain moved, and I saw a flash of skin. What was going on in there?

The unmarked Impala turned the corner, and Barr pulled up behind me. His boots hit the pavement, and he strode to my side.

"Anything?"

"Curtains are closed in the front room. One of them moved a second ago. At least I think so."

"I called for backup, just in case. Sergeant Zahn himself is coming."

"So now we just wait?"

He nodded. "Tell me about Cabot Reyes."

"Well, I know she was one of Elizabeth's clients. I don't think Dorothy knew she was seeing a therapist, though, because otherwise she would've put two and two together earlier. After all, Dorothy has known about all the skeletons in her family for a long time. I had to ferret them out."

And she'd gone to Caladia Acres for

lunch. If Felix had asked her how much money Cabot got when Dorothy died, I was going to kill that sweet old leprechaun.

"Why would Reyes kill Quentin Swenson?" Barr asked.

I frowned. "Same motive the rest of the Swensons had: money. And if that was her motive, she had ample opportunity." I ticked off the reasons on my fingers. "She's a nurse, so she knows how to use poison to induce a heart attack. She had access to Victoria's herb garden. She could have known about the poison hemlock growing there. She had access to any number of bottles of mead and could easily have added the poison."

"There have to be other ways to cause a heart attack," Barr said, eyes never leaving the Dorothy's house.

"True. But the poison hemlock isn't a drug that could be traced to her profession. And if anyone got suspicious, Victoria or Willa would likely be blamed, not Cabot."

"But Cabot was the only one of them who was Elizabeth's client," he said.

I nodded. "If no one had heard Elizabeth's tape, she would have gotten away with it." The street was quiet. "How soon will Zahn get here?"

"Any —"

A gunshot split the air. It came from Dorothy Swenson's house.

Barr took off running. I half-limped, half-loped across the lawn right behind him while my mind scrambled to catch up with the idea of gunplay. *Gunplay.* Of all the stupid developments. Poisoners and shooters were at opposite ends of the spectrum when it came to violence. In theory at least.

Obviously, not in practice. Not today. Dorothy Swenson wasn't the easiest or nicest person in the world, but she was in a wheelchair, for crying in a bucket. Had Cabot just shot her in cold blood?

"Stay back," Barr ordered when we got as far as the yard.

I nodded, hugging the wall to the left of the front door.

He gave me a look that indicated perhaps he had meant for me to stay farther back than that.

Well, I wasn't going to move now. Someone in there had a gun. And my ankle hurt.

He stood to the other side of the door and banged on it with his fist. "Police! Open up!" His weapon was in his other hand.

Given the circumstances, it was probably wrong of me to feel a giddy thrill at seeing him like that. The pointy-toed boots and Western string tie gave him the look of an old-timey marshal. The expression on his chiseled features made me glad he was on my side.

Across the street, three people had gathered. They murmured and stared at the cowboy with the gun and the disheveled limping wonder squeezed up tight against the gray siding. Another man joined them. Pretty soon there'd be a real gawker knot.

Where the heck were Sergeant Zahn and his merry crew?

"Enter!" The barked word could have come from no other throat than Dorothy Swenson's.

Barr raised perplexed eyebrows at me. I shrugged, wide-eyed.

"Detective! Enter!" Dorothy demanded.

He reached out a hesitant hand and turned the knob. Pushed the door in, still standing to the side.

"If you don't get in here this instant, I'm going to shoot her right between the eyes."

He peered slowly around the door. "Ma'am. No more shooting, please."

"Nonsense. Is that your wife out there?"

"Yes, ma'am," I called.

Barr glared at me. This time the expression on his chiseled features made me *hope* he was on my side.

"You get in here, too."

"Why?" Barr asked, his voice reasonable. "She doesn't have anything to do with this."

"Poppycock!"

The gun went off again, louder than before, sending me half a foot into the air. Back on land, my heart kept right on jumping, my ears rang, and my ankle throbbed.

Lucky for us, Dorothy's voice could cut right through hearing loss. "Enter!"

Barr straightened and walked inside, gun pointed at someone in the living room.

I followed.

Cabot Reyes sat on the sofa, arms straight by her sides like a pinned butterfly. Her dark, terrified eyes flew from Barr to me and back to Barr. I could smell the fear rolling off her. It mingled with the dust and doilies and old lady perfume in the dim curtained daylight.

But my husband was pointing his gun at the little old lady who sat across from her in the wheelchair. Who also had a gun. A rather big one, actually, resting in her lap but trained on her nurse companion.

She glanced up at Barr. "Put that thing down."

"You first," he said.

Her laugh was bitter. "No deal. This woman killed my grandson. She's about to confess that to you."

"How about if she comes down to the station to do that?"

Dorothy considered. "I don't think she'll do it then. If she doesn't confess now, I'll just have to kill her."

A car screeched to a stop outside. *Great timing, Sergeant.* I hoped they wouldn't come barreling into the house. Someone — everyone — was bound to get shot then.

"We know Cabot killed Quentin," I said, stepping forward.

Both women turned their heads toward me.

"We know she put poison hemlock in a bottle of mead, allowing the wine to leach out the toxins."

Something flickered in Cabot's bird eyes that told me I was right so far.

"Then she removed the plant and put another shrink-wrap seal over the flip-top closure."

Cabot's chin swung back and forth in denial. "You can't prove that. I'm telling you, it wasn't me."

"Did Iris take mead home for her husband on a regular basis? Did he have a favorite?"

The nurse was silent.

Dorothy said, "Yes, she took two bottles of sage blossom mead home for him every week. I often saw them in her office on

327

Friday afternoons before she left for the weekend."

"Providing you plenty of opportunity to switch one with your evil brew," I said to Cabot. "What if Iris had shared a drink with Quentin that night? Or is that what you were hoping for?"

"No, she . . ." Her mouth snapped shut.

"Iris prefers sweet mead to dry," Dorothy said.

"Well, at least there's that." I pointed. "So you had the knowhow and the opportunity. And you were Elizabeth Moser's psychotherapy client. You told her the only solution to your problem was to kill someone."

Cabot's eyes filled.

"But Elizabeth didn't name the victim. If we'd known, perhaps we could have saved him." I looked down at Dorothy. "I'm sorry."

She didn't answer, but she didn't look like she wanted to shoot me, either.

"But she had to tell the police, Cabot. Had to tell your potential victim. She had no choice. And where did that leave you?"

The tears spilled, twin streaks down her cheeks. "With no choice."

"You had to kill her."

Her throat worked.

"At least it was good practice," I said. "For

the main event."

"Ambrose! You in there?" Sergeant Zahn banged on the door. Couldn't anyone just knock politely?

"No one else!" Dorothy said. "Let your wife finish!"

Cabot looked less than pleased at that.

Barr and I exchanged looks. He nodded. "I'll just go have a word with my boss."

"No." Dorothy shook her head. "You'll let him in. He can come in when we're done here. Not before."

When we're done here? That sounded ominous.

"If I don't talk to him, he'll break the door down," Barr said.

Dorothy responded with a withering look. "Call him."

If you could dial a phone wryly, that's what my husband did. "Sergeant? Hold off a bit. Things are a bit . . . volatile . . . in here." A pause. "No sir. No wounded . . . Yes, two shots." His eyes raked the walls, stopped near the ceiling above the sofa. "In the wall board, I'd say . . . Let's make it fifteen. Okay. Yessir."

He flipped his phone closed and put it in his pocket. "Happy?"

Dorothy snorted. "Hardly. So the SWAT team will tear down the house in fifteen

329

minutes?"

"Something like that." Barr still pointed his gun at the wheelchair, but I could see the set of his shoulders had relaxed the tiniest bit.

"So anyway," I said to Cabot. "You stole your file — and a bunch of others — after you killed your therapist."

Poor Elizabeth, deciding to have a glass of mead before contacting the authorities about her murderous client. I wondered whether she'd realized her mistake as she lay dying, waiting for her pizza to arrive.

"How did you manage to poison her mead?"

Cabot pressed her lips together. For such a tall woman, she had shrunk far down into the sofa cushions.

"You know Elizabeth made verbal notes on cassette tapes, and she kept them separate from her paper files." I leaned forward. "What we haven't told anyone is that we've tracked down another tape where she talks about you. Specifically. By name."

Falsehood is perfectly permissible when soliciting a confession. Barr had taught me that much. Practice and more practice had taught me how to lie. The trick was to stick as close to the truth as you could.

"So, we know you did it," I said. "Whether

330

you confess or Dorothy here just shoots you, we already know enough."

Cabot blinked.

Barr's gaze snagged mine for an instant. Something in it. Approval, maybe. Or perhaps just amusement.

I crossed my arms. "The thing I want to know is why you did it."

The tears on her cheeks had dried, but her laugh was a little unsteady. "You really think I'm going to talk to you in here, like this?"

Dorothy raised the gun and pointed it straight at her nurse's chest. She had remarkable upper body strength for an octogenarian. Then I caught the look on her face. She was serious; she'd happily execute Cabot Reyes and suffer the consequences.

Cabot saw it, too. Her face crumpled. "I killed Quentin because I couldn't kill you, Dorothy."

THIRTY-TWO

What?

Confused, we all waited for her to continue. Finally, she did. "I'm your nurse. If there was any suspicion at all regarding your death, it would fall on me first."

Fury ripped across Dorothy's lined face. "You little worm. This was about *money?*"

"You're in Dorothy's will," I said. "Of course."

"Not anymore, she's not!"

"Dorothy," I admonished. "I think that kind of goes without saying, don't you?"

She grimaced. Put the gun back in her lap — still pointing toward the sofa.

"How much would she get?" I asked Dorothy. "An equal share?"

"Of course not. She's not family. But I did value her service. I would have left her seven percent of my liquid assets."

"And you're worth, what, four million? Seven percent is a lot to kill for."

Cabot snorted. "She not worth that anymore. Another year and she wouldn't have had a dime left."

Her employer glared at her. "You horrible, selfish woman. That's why you killed my grandson? To stop me from helping him?"

I squinted. "I don't understand."

Barr said, "The civil suit against Quentin."

"It was costing a fortune." Cabot's eyes pleaded with us to understand. "The court case would have gone on forever. She'd have spent all her money trying to save his reputation."

"So . . . get rid of Quentin, which gets rid of the lawsuit, and you get your seven percent of millions instead of nothing in the long run."

Cabot looked relieved that I understood.

"Funny how none of her grandchildren felt that desperate." I began to pace. Stopped when I almost walked in front of Barr's gun.

He looked irritated.

"That's because they aren't that desperate," Cabot said. "Not like me. They all have other income. Spouses. Jobs with benefits. A piece of the meadery. I have nothing. *Nothing.* You think this woman provides health care or a retirement plan?"

Dorothy waved the gun. "Bah. You're healthy as a horse. And I pay you well. Should have saved up better."

Cabot stood. "You paid me crap."

"Sit down," Barr said, the words sharp.

She sat back down. "You paid me a pittance, always saying how I had room and board on top of my wages."

"You did. For fifteen years I gave you a place to stay and food to eat."

"I'm not a stray dog. And you think it's so great living here with you? I was going to get a tiny fraction of what your grandkids were going to inherit, but did they have to put up with your nastiness day in and day out?"

Dorothy opened her mouth.

Cabot ran roughshod over her. "No, they did not. They had to put up with you all right, but in dribs and drabs, in tiny little increments. And they didn't have to do any of the hard work, either. You gave me a roof and food? I bathed you, dressed you, cooked for you, cleaned this mausoleum. I put you to bed at night, was at your beck and call twenty-four seven. I had no life of my own."

Dorothy stared at her. "I thought . . . I thought we were friends."

"You're a mean old piece of work who demands everything and gives nothing.

Friends? Has the dementia finally set in?"

Oh, gosh. I felt bad for Dorothy. I felt bad for Cabot. But maybe they were like one of those dysfunctional couples who stay together out of spite.

"Why didn't you leave, get another job?" Barr asked.

"Because I couldn't. I'm too old to start a new career. Even if I found another nursing job, I wouldn't have any security. I needed that money she promised over and over, in order to survive my retirement with any kind of dignity."

Barr looked at his watch. Our fifteen minutes of infamy were almost over.

"Was Elizabeth Moser your friend?" I asked.

Cabot's eyes filled. "I thought so. I don't have very many friends, and it was so nice to have someone to talk to. I went to her because I was so unhappy, so worried all the time. She helped me understand I wasn't a victim. That I was in control of my own life. Then she had to go do that."

"Betray you?"

She nodded. "I had to do it. Don't you see? I had to kill her. I'd introduced her to mead, and I knew she bought it from A Fine Body and had a glass when she got home from work. See, she told me things like that.

That's what friends do. So I sneaked into her house when I knew she was at the Blackwell Building and replaced the contents of the bottle she had open in the refrigerator. I knew she'd drink it that night. It was so easy. She didn't even bother to lock her back door."

We were all quiet for a long moment, the air in the dark living room heavy with confession, desperation, and hatred. I didn't want to breathe it in anymore.

"Time's up," Barr said. "Anything else you want to say?"

"Yes." Dorothy held her gun up to him. He extracted it carefully from her grasp. "I'm sorry I was so difficult to live with. I had no idea. Thank you for bringing it to my attention."

I blinked.

She inclined her white head. "And I hope you rot in hell for what you did to my grandson and the woman you considered a friend."

Cabot started to cry again.

"Sergeant!" Dorothy barked. "Enter!"

No SWAT team waited outside, only Sergeant Zahn and two patrolmen. Cabot went quietly with the officer Sergeant Zahn assigned to take her to the station. Willa had joined the growing number of people across the street and thumped over to her grandmother on her crutches as soon as we all emerged.

"Are you okay? What happened?"

Dorothy patted Willa on the hand. "Cabot killed Quentin. Call a family meeting, and I'll tell you all about it." She looked up at Barr. "Are you going to arrest me?"

He smiled. "We have to charge you, but I don't know that we have to hold you in jail or anything. Where'd you get the gun?"

"My brother gave it to me. He has a lot of them."

Of course he did.

"Who will take care of you now?" I asked.

"I will," Willa answered. "And Victoria and Glenwood, until another nurse can be found. After all, Grandmother has always taken good care of us."

Barr drew me aside. "I'll need you to come down and make a statement."

"I'll come right away, while everything is still fresh."

"Don't worry," he said, and held out his hand. It held a mini-cassette.

"Is that . . . ?"

He nodded. "I taped the whole thing. On one of Elizabeth Moser's blank cassettes."

■ ■ ■ ■

While Cabot had been confessing, the multi-jurisdictional team had been busy. That night Meghan, Erin, Barr, and I sat around the butcher block table eating grilled salmon, asparagus, and wild rice pilaf while my husband filled us in.

"Robin cracked one of the delivery drivers," he said. "He gave Normal Brown up completely. Now that Jakie is dead, Normal doesn't have an enforcer, and folks aren't as afraid of him as they once were."

"That's terrific," Meghan said. She was up to speed on what had been going on the last week and was only mildly peeved at my antics during her absence. "Can you build a good case against him now?"

"Oh, more than good. Once the first driver started talking, two others jumped right in. From what we can tell so far, the old man threatened and blackmailed them into bringing marijuana in from Canada when they delivered mead up there. Dorothy found out and stopped it, but Normal started right back up after a few weeks, even though he told her he'd stopped. The drivers are willing to testify against him."

"So he'll go to jail?" Erin asked.

"Oh, yeah. Plus, we raided the house where Jakie nabbed you and found a full-blown meth lab. With Normal in it. He's toast."

"As long as the drugs aren't getting into the schools anymore," Meghan said.

"What about Jakie?" I asked.

"We're testing all of Normal's guns for ballistics. I'm hoping we can find a match for the bullet in Jakie's chest."

"Don't forget the gun he gave Dorothy," I said.

"I thought of that. The caliber is right, too. I wouldn't be surprised if that old bastard offloaded a murder weapon on his sister."

"Not to change the subject," Meghan said. "But I have some news to share."

I set my fork down. "Does it have to do with Mr. O'Connell?"

"It does." She flashed white teeth in a big grin.

Erin's eyes got big. "Are you getting married, Mom?"

Meghan cocked her head. "Do you think we should?"

One slim shoulder rose and fell. "I dunno. Do you want to? I mean, like, do you love him?"

My housemate slowly nodded. "Yes, I love

him. But no, we're not getting married. Not yet. He's going to move to Cadyville next month, though. So we can see what it's like to actually live in the same town."

"A step in the right direction," Barr said.

"And about bloody time," I said.

Erin sat in the middle of the living room on Sunday afternoon, surrounded by shreds of wrapping paper and a circle of admiring adults. That night there would be a party with her friends at the roller rink, but the afternoon was for us. Tootie and Felix were there, along with Barr and Meghan and me. And Zoe had the privilege of attending both parties.

Barr handed Tootie a jar.

"What's this?" she asked.

"Victoria's tea," I said. "The crime lab says it's exactly what she said. Black cohosh, meadowsweet, yarrow, and bogbean, with enough peppermint to make it palatable. Knock yourself out."

"Thank you. I like to think it really helped my arthritis."

"And she's still selling it, so let me know if you want more," I said.

"Time for cake!" Meghan announced, carrying in the lemon cheesecake she'd made that morning, twelve candles flickering on top.

We warbled "Happy Birthday" with varying degrees of vocal ability as Erin jumped up and followed her to the coffee table. When we were done, she grinned at all of us and then looked up at the ceiling, thinking. Then, with one decisive dip of her head, she blew out all the candles.

Meghan cut the cake and Erin distributed plates. Soon we were all seated on cushion, floor, or hearth, and for several seconds the only sounds were the clinking of forks against stoneware.

"I've decided what my book is going to be about," Erin said between bites.

I set my cake down. "Can you tell us? Or will that interfere with your creative process?"

"Nah, I can tell you. See, there's this girl. She's, like, twelve or so. And she has a secret fairy godmother who comes and visits her in her dreams. One night she tells the girl she has to save a golden horse."

"Cool," Zoe said.

"Yeah. So anyways, she goes to find the golden horse in her dreams. In real life she goes into like a — what do you call them? When you don't wake up?"

"A coma," Meghan said.

"Right. A coma. But in the dream place where her fairy godmother lives she goes looking for the golden horse and she meets all these new friends. There's a talking dragonfly, and a crazy bird lady, and a bunch of flower fairies, and a prince with blond hair and blue eyes."

She leaned over to Zoe. "He looks just like Justin Scott."

"Ooh! He's cute."

"Right. So they aren't the only ones trying to find the horse. There's a big ol' giant and a little bitty gnome, and they want the horse, too. Only they want to chop it up and sell it — it's really made of gold, see — but the girl and her friends want to save the horse's life."

She beamed at all of us. "I'm going to write it in the journal Sophie Mae gave me." She held up the red leather blank book I'd found at Kringle's.

Everyone started talking about the girl and the golden horse. I leaned over to Barr, sitting beside me on the sofa. "*That's* what she got out of all those notes she was taking? It has nothing to do with anything that happened last week."

The look he gave me was full of exaggerated pity. "I guess you just don't understand the creative process."

I punched him in the arm.

"She's pretty amazing," he said. "Do you think you might want one?"

"What, a twelve-year-old?" I joked. "I think one is enough."

"No. Not a twelve-year-old. Do you want to have a baby?"

"Oh. Um, I . . . maybe. We should talk about it, huh."

He put his hand on my knee and squeezed. "I think so."

I really didn't know if I wanted a baby or not. But the clock over the fireplace mantle suddenly seemed very loud.

Tick, tock. Tick, tock.

RECIPES

REFRESHING BATH MELTS

These are a simple combination of blooming bath oil and bath bombs. The essential oil blend is a great pick-me-up and works well to clear a stuffy nose. Of course you can substitute any other essential oil you like. Be sure whatever you use is safe for your skin. Lavender and tea tree are almost universally tolerated. You can also experiment with the butter (shea and cocoa butter are both nice).

1/2 cup citric acid
1/2 cup baking soda
1/2 cup mango butter
1/4 teaspoon each of peppermint, eucalyptus, tea tree, and rosemary essential oils
2 tablespoons Polysorbate 20 (optional)

Thoroughly mix citric acid and baking soda together. Slowly melt the butter in the microwave or over a double boiler. Stir in essential oil and the Polysorbate 20 if you're using it, then mix with the citric acid and baking soda. Spoon into small molds, being sure to eliminate any air pockets. Place into freezer to harden quickly. Unmold only after the bath melts are completely cold.

Polysorbate 20 is an emulsifier that disperses the oil into the water so it will rinse cleanly down the drain. It's derived from lauric acid and is considered a nonionic surfactant.

You can buy Polysorbate 20 a number of places online, including www.snowdrift farm.com. However, if you don't want to bother, dislike the idea of putting a chemical in your bath melts, and don't mind a little oil left in the tub, you can just leave it out.

PEPPERMINT SUGAR SCRUB

Sugar cane produces glycolic acid, which is a natural alpha hydroxyl acid. That, plus the sugar crystals, exfoliate skin to leave it wonderfully soft. It's nice for your face, but you might find you want to use it all over. You can use any oil you want to, though jojoba oil most closely mimics the oils our skin produce. Avocado or plain old olive oil work well, too. If you have sensitive skin or acne, replace the peppermint oil with lavender and/or tea tree oil. If you have oily skin, replace the oil with liquid glycerin.

1 part white cane sugar
1 part oil
Peppermint essential oil (about 1/4 teaspoon
    per cup of mixture to start)

Combine ingredients thoroughly, slather on and let sit for three or four minutes. You'll feel your skin tighten a bit, as with a mask. If you wish, rub gently to exfoliate and then rinse thoroughly.

HOMEMADE GINGER BEER

This can be a tricky endeavor as the idea is to harness yeasts which occur naturally in the air to ferment your ginger culture. Certain areas naturally have more yeasts than others (like the distinctive San Francisco sourdough) as do some kitchens. But don't be intimidated, as it's a simple process and doesn't take many ingredients or special equipment. Always make sure your jars, bottles, and utensils are perfectly clean to start with. Read the whole recipe through before you begin so you can see what you'll need to have on hand.

First you have to make the culture, which is what Tootie teaches Erin how to do. Simply add a teaspoon of either powdered ginger or chopped ginger root to a teaspoon of sugar and a cup and a half of filtered or spring water. Mix together in a wide-mouthed canning jar and cover with a single layer of cheesecloth. You want it to have plenty of access to the air. Let it sit on the kitchen counter for twenty-four hours or so.

Then for the next seven days add another teaspoon of sugar and one of ginger each day and mix thoroughly. If you start with chopped ginger root, don't switch to powder and vice versa. You are feeding your ginger culture during this week. After a few days it should start to form little bubbles. That means it's fermenting!

On the last day, strain the mixture through a piece of muslin or an old, clean dish towel. Discard the solids (or save them to start another batch) and put the liquid in a bowl or pan that can accommodate seven or more quarts of liquid. Mix in 5 quarts of filtered or spring water, 3 cups of sugar and the juice of two or three lemons. Stir until the sugar dissolves.

Then get out your funnel and the plastic water or soda bottles you've saved and carefully washed with hot soapy water, rinsed thoroughly and allowed to dry. Any size works, just make sure you have enough to hold up to 7 quarts. Using plastic rather than glass helps avoid the exploding bottle problem Barr's mother had with her root beer. Be sure to wash the caps as well.

Fill the bottles, leaving a few inches at the top for the gases to expand as your ginger beer continues to ferment. Twist on the caps. Let the bottles sit at room temperature for two days, checking them often. When you see bubbles forming, put the bottles in the fridge immediately. Your ginger beer is ready to drink! Some bottles may ferment faster than others, especially if you use different sizes. Be careful not to allow any to ferment too long or the pressure inside will spray the contents out when you open it.

If any alcohol forms during the fermentation it is negligible and very diluted at the end, so this drink is suitable for children and adults alike.

ABOUT THE AUTHOR

Cricket McRae's interest in traditional colonial skills is reflected in her contemporary Home Crafting Mysteries. Set in the Pacific Northwest, they feature everything from soap making to food preservation, spinning to cheese making. For recipes and more information about Cricket, go to her website, www.cricketmcrae.com, or her blog, www.hearthcricket.com.

We hope you have enjoyed this Large Print book. Other Thorndike, Wheeler, Kennebec, and Chivers Press Large Print books are available at your library or directly from the publishers.

For information about current and upcoming titles, please call or write, without obligation, to:

Publisher
Thorndike Press
10 Water St., Suite 310
Waterville, ME 04901
Tel. (800) 223-1244

or visit our Web site at:

http://gale.cengage.com/thorndike

OR

Chivers Large Print
published by AudioGO Ltd
St James House, The Square
Lower Bristol Road
Bath BA2 3SB
England
Tel. +44(0) 800 136919
email: info@audiogo.co.uk
www.audiogo.co.uk

All our Large Print titles are designed for easy reading, and all our books are made to last.